Lock Down Publications and Ca$h
Presents

STAY DANGEROUS

A PORTLAND TALE

Written By

FOREIGN BOOMIN

First Edition 2025

Printed in the United States of America

Lock Down Publications
P.O. Box 944
Stockbridge, GA 30281
www.lockdownpublications.com

Like our page on Facebook: Lock Down Publications
www.facebook.com/lockdownpublications.ldp

Stay Connected with Us!

Text **LOCKDOWN** to 22828 to stay up-to-date with new releases, sneak peaks, contests and more…

Like our page on Facebook:
Lock Down Publications

Join Lock Down Publications/The New Era Reading Group

Visit our website:
www.lockdownpublications.com

Follow us on Instagram:
Lock Down Publications

Email Us: We want to hear from you!

Statement

Stay Dangerous is by no means a justification for gang involvement, or crime. Nor is it intended in anyway as the confession of one person's crimes. Stay Dangerous is the story of a lifestyle and the destruction it creates.

Chapter 1

Life's a trip, Los thought as he sat in silence, enjoying the solitude he learned to love. In a life plagued by chaos, the moments of peace were appreciated, however rare they were.

No niggas with hidden agendas calling him, no nagging-ass bitch bothering him, regardless of her good intentions.

He looked down at the Glock in his lap and the 50k on the couch next to him. Blood money. He hit the Backwood and inhaled the Gelato smoke as he laughed at the irony of this shit. They say "Money buys happiness," but the price you pay with your soul to acquire it ain't a cheap one.

"Fuck it," he said out loud to no one, as he set the blunt in the ashtray then rose from the sectional and went to put the money up. He took off his black Nike tech sweatsuit and threw it in the washer to get rid of any DNA on it, then hopped in the shower to do the same for his body. He would still get rid of the sweatsuit when he left. Can't never be too careful.

"Gotta work smarter, not harder," his pops used to tell him. And if he never listened to shit, he listened to that shit!

***

"Solo in my Benzo, flying down the highway, solitary thoughts like how to reinvest my side change." Nipsey Hussle preached through the speakers as Los pushed down Stark Street in his own foreign.

Middle of the summer and boy, it was a hot one! Bodies was dropping every day. Bitches was lining niggas up for a bag, and it was definitely friendly fire with the homies! You couldn't trust no nigga and definitely couldn't love no bitch.

He pulled into the apartments on 150th and Stark and backed into the parking spot. His brother Juice got out of the Camaro next to him and hopped in his shit. His right-hand man. From pots and pans to a hunnid grand!

Originally from Alberta Park Mobb, they fell back when shit started getting watered down. Niggas wasn't in the field, they was on the internet! They linked with Los' relative Kapone from North Vegas and started M.A.F.I.A.—Money And Family In Action. Get some money or catch a body was the only thing they endorsed. It was money over most but loyalty overall.

"What's bracking, brother? You got the blanks with you?" Juice asked after they shook each other up.

"You already know I'm not tryna see Krystal old annoying ass for these checks."

"Duh, foo. I almost forgot the cards but we good. After we drop, we finna cash advance out every dollar from every account 'til they flag them muthafuckas," Los said.

Juice nodded his head and rubbed his hands together like Birdman.

"My muthafucking nigga!" he said, and they both laughed and thought about the smooth 30k they would split today.

Scamming, fraud, couch hustling. Whatever you wanted to call it. They were all for it. The only niggas hating was the broke ones! Besides catching COVID a few times, the pandemic had definitely been good to them!

Grab a few Pro's off Telegram and BOOM! COVID relief, unemployment, and PPP loans in 9–10 different names. Excuse them for working smarter, not harder! This shit was a non-contact sport. Niggas went from Buicks to Benzes, and bitches' asses went from unappealing to Brazilian!

Later that night

"Double up on red," Los told the dealer as he put ten $500 chips down.

"My nigga, you tripping. Take that shit and go," Juice told him as they stood at the roulette table at Ilani Casino.

"Scary money don't make money, my boy! This shit free bands!" Los responded as they watched the wheel spin and the ball bounce... and land on a red number! "Like I said! Pay me my money!" Los yelled. He was on a hot streak turning $100 into 10k. The dealer looked at him salty when he walked off with all his chips. He cashed out, and as they were heading to the exit, he saw a bitch-ass nigga. "There go that nigga Paul. I think he finna leave too."

"On my mama," Juice said back to him. "We on his ass!"

They got to the car, Los put the magnetic covers over each license plate, then drove to the exit and waited for him. Now the logical thing would be to give this sucka a pass. They had 40k in the car between the two of them—why not go home? Hennessy and enemies, one hell of a mixture!

"There go the nigga in the black Durango! Let's go," Juice said, ready to drill a nigga. Los waited a few seconds after he passed them and pulled off. It was 3 a.m., they were the only two cars on the freeway this far from the town. "Pull up next to him. I'm finna flip his load!" Juice flipped the switch on his Glizzy, turning it into a fully. He had a see-through 40 stalk hanging out the bottom. Their phones were already turned off.

Juice rolled his window down as Los pulled up right next to the Durango and started shooting into the driver's window.

WOP! WOP! WOP! WOP! WOP! He hit that nigga and the Durango started swerving. They were both going 90 mph, the Durango kept swerving out of control. Juice aimed for the front tire and squeezed!

WOP! WOP! WOP! WOP! WOP! The bullets shredded the tire, it swerved again and flipped!

It slid sideways, upside down into a ditch. If the Glizzy aint kill him, that did. Los put the 745i in sport mode and did the dash outta there!

***

"Aye, I'm getting a dope-ass Airbnb in Phoenix the next two weeks, you tryna hit the road?" Juice asked Los before he got out the car.

"Shit, I got a few plays lined up next week. I'll let you know wassup though," Los said.

"Bet, brother," Juice told him, then hopped out. "Stay dangerous, foo."

"Yup. I'ma get with you," Los said back to him and pulled off. *What a muthafucking day*, he thought as he drove home.

Chapter 2

"Aye! Fuck it up, bitch!" Kaleah yelled as she recorded her sister Liv twerkin in the front seat at the red light. They laughed as the light turned green and sped off.

Kaleah and Liv. Both Black and Japanese. Both been under Dr. Miami's knife. Both bad and both touching more money than most of these niggas. High-class Portland bitches.

"Let me see that shit again," Liv said to her sister. "Bitch, I can't believe you inked his name on your face! I love it though. A ghetto love story."

"Bitch, you better believe it! The nigga loves me—loves me! Plus, he got my shit first. I love that energy. 'Tat my name, baby, so I know it's real,'" Kaleah started singing like Drake.

"Sis, if you like it, I love it! Shit, my nigga got some catching up to do. Niggas out here getting bitches' names on they face! Whaaat! I get a Gucci bag... the small one. I hate it here." Liv made a what-the-fuck face and they started laughing.

Kaleah's commitment to Los was solid and unbreakable. His words knocked her, his actions kept her, but the way he stimulated her—not only physically but mentally—had her in love. They were each other's peace. And they shared love and loyalty.

Later that night

"Babe, have you eaten today?" Kaleah asked as the server brought them their drinks.

Damn, I love a bitch that care, Los thought, but said, "Nah, I been busy, but shit, fuck that food," then knocked back his tequila shot.

I'ma feed, fuck, and love this nigga for the rest of my life, Kaleah promised herself.

Just a few months into their relationship and they moved and treated each other as if they had already spent lifetimes together before this one. Soul ties.

"I'm finna eat some pussy later though," Los smiled at her and said, then started rapping Lil Baby at the table: *"Come and put that pussy on me, don't be running from me,"* then winked at her.

"I know that's right! Sucking toes, ass, all that shit!" she said back to him, and they both started cracking up at the table. Energy.

Their chemistry was on ten, and the way they vibed off each other only enhanced it.

Kaleah knocked her shot back and said, "Babe, let's get our food to go and just chill at home."

Los shook his head and smiled. "Why you so nasty, Lee? You just tryna go home and get your ass ate."

She winked at him and smiled back. "Fuck that food, remember? Come on, get the check. We can get a bottle on the way home." Then she was up and out the door.

This freaky-ass bitch, Los thought to himself and smiled. He laid a $50 bill down for the drinks, leaving before the food arrived.

***

"Bitch, you know who shot you, now come get it back in blood!" Kaleah rapped with Pooh Shiesty as the song played, recording herself on Snapchat. She put her phone down and looked at Los as he drove.

"Babe, do you love me?" she asked him.

"Huh?" he said back to her, caught off guard by the random question.

"Nigga, you heard me. Do you love me?"

DING. DING. DING. DING. DING. DING. DING.

"Man, put yo seatbelt on. That shit is annoying as fuck," Los told her, changing the subject.

She was fully turned in her seat now, facing him. She reached over and turned the music off. All eyes on him. "Hellooo, sir. Do I need to repeat myself?" she asked.

"Man. Why you tryna fuck up a good night?" Los said to her.

"Fuck up a good night, huh," Kaleah said with an attitude. "So tell me why the fuck Liv's boyfriend told her he saw you at the gas station with that Mexican bitch Maria in your car? This same car we're in right now, actually!" She yelled the last part.

Maria? he thought. *Was I slipping with that bitch in the load?* But he said, "That nigga's high. You're tripping."

"So that's a no then?" she asked him.

"That's a fuck no," he responded but made a mental note to ask that nigga why he was pillow-talking about him.

"I know, baby, I was capping. I just always wanted to do some ghetto shit like that," she said and smiled at him.

He looked at her and said nothing for a few seconds, then, "Bitch, you're toxic."

"Oooh, daddy, so toxic. My pussy is so wet," she said to him, then took his hand and put it in her leggings and guided his finger into her, and breathed in hard when he moved it in and out. Then she took his hand back out and looked at him as she put his finger in her mouth, sucking the juices off of it. "Daddy, why we still at the light? Get me home," she whined, then slipped her hand into her pants and got busy. With the music off, it sounded like she was stirring macaroni.

He put his foot on the gas and ran the red light, and he broke every traffic law on the way home. *Fuck it.*

***

"I thought you was my nigga," the person said, staring up at the man pointing the gun at him.

"Yeah? And I thought you was a real nigga. We was both wrong."

BAKA! BAKA! BAKA! BAKA! BAKA! BAKA!

The shots rang out, violently waking Los up from the nightmare in a cold sweat.

"Relax, babe. You're home safe with me. Take a deep breath, please," Kaleah comforted him. The tossing and turning had woke her too.

"Fuck," he said in between breaths, wiping the sweat from his forehead.

"You wanna talk about it?" she asked him. "You might have PTSD, babe. That shit is real. I'm concerned about you."

She felt his pain, and he felt the love pouring from her.

Los looked around the room. At the TV on the wall. The full-length mirrors on each side of the bed frame, and at the door to the walk-in closet, and pictured everything they had in it.

He knew he could never give up this life with her. He also knew that to secure their future, he had to bury the demons in his past.

FLASHBACK

"My nigga, the hoes in here going crazy!" Juice said, looking around the mansion Airbnb.

"Dead homies! And we them muthafucking niggas in this bitch!" Los told him as he shook the bottle of Belaire and sprayed it on a group of strippers' ass cheeks twerking on the pool table.

Los wasn't lying. Standing at 6'2" with a slim build, green eyes, and the tan skin he got from his West Indian parents always had a bad bitch shooting her shot.

Tonight, he had on a black Gucci crewneck sweater, Gucci belt, skinny Purple Label jeans, and red Balenciaga no-laces. His neck and ears were buss down. He was easily the flyest in the building.

"Trust me, bro, this shit regular. This just the beginning, my boy! We was on that yard—I told you when you came home you was gon' ball with' me! We finna go on a muthafucking run this summer!" Los told Juice. "Shaq and Penny, balling heavy! You muthafucking feel me!" he yelled over the music, then drank what was left of the Belaire and left the empty bottle on the pool table.

He checked his Apple Watch. 2:45 a.m.

"Let's get the fuck outta here though. These sweaty bitches is low budget, and it's way badder bitches on the strip."

"Yup. Boom and them niggas at Planet Hollywood right now," Juice told him.

"Bet. Text Blood we on the way," Los said back to him. Then he looked around the private party they were at. He saw niggas grouping up, whispering to each other.

That was the downside of being outta town and shitting on the local niggas. Especially dusty Vegas niggas. The bitches loved it and the niggas hated.

"These nerd-ass niggas not slick," he thought to himself.

He knew a gun didn't make you a killer. It just gave you the upper hand.

Los and Juice fasho had the upper hand.

They got outside and instantly clutched pole. Even if the powder just had him paranoid, he rather be judged by 12 than carried by 6.

One up top and Glocks aint got no safety.

They turned the corner a block from the party and were 100 feet from the car when two suckas from the party jumped out the bushes and said, "Bitch nigga, run all that shit!" pointing to Los and Juice's jewelry.

Was intimidation their weapon? This must've been their first time—or they thought they had an easy lick—because there wasn't a gun in either of their hands.

Shame on their older homies for sending them outside with no gun to rob a killer!

WOP! WOP! WOP! WOP! WOP! WOP! WOP!

Shots rang out in Henderson that night and two local niggas choked tryna bite off more than they could chew!

Los pressed the remote start on his fob while they ran to the car. They hopped in and did the dash, hearing the sirens in the distance.

As they got on the freeway towards Vegas and away from the sirens, they started laughing. The adrenaline had them high as fuck.

They both caught a body back there.

"Fuck them dead niggas," Los said. "We in this shit forever, nigga!"

Nothing more needed to be said. They shook hands and knew they were all in.

Chapter 3

DING!

"5 pm Gateway Fred Meyers parking lot. 10 boats. 10k"

The message Los just received on Telegram was exactly what he was waiting for. 10 boats. 10 thousand dollars. Shit, an easy 40k profit. 30's, blues, pressies, fetty. Whatever you wanted to call them had the streets going crazy! And Los was definitely contributing to the opioid epidemic. If not him, it was going to be somebody else. And what he look like letting the next nigga score when he could be winning?

He liked to have his hand in everything. One income was too close to none income and that broke shit wasn't for him! Trapping, macking, scamming. And if shit got heavy, he was running in that spot with the ski mask!

He pulled up to the spot and viewed his surroundings.

DING! Los opened up Telegram: *"Black truck."* And there it was. He put the Glock 20 in the pocket of the Moncler jacket he was wearing then got out of his car and got in the truck.

"Why Bird not here?" Los immediately asked the Mexican sitting in the driver's seat.

"I'm his brother. He couldn't make it. From now on I'll be doing the drops with you. I'm Eddy."

Los was definitely finna holla at Bird later about this but said, "long as the business is good, I'm good." Words that would jinx him moments later.

"You got the 10 G's?" Eddy asked him and handed over the sealed paint can.

"Like I said, good business," Los said then handed him the knot of money. The can felt lighter than it normally did so he started to pop the top off.

"Do that on your own time, holmes. I got places to be," Eddy said quickly. A lil too quickly.

As he said that bullshit, Los popped the top off and looked inside. It was short 5 bags. 5 boats.

"Where the other half of my shit?" Los snapped. And this is where Eddy had him fucked up.

"Your deal with my brother was 10 for 10. The deal with me is 10k for 5 boats. But the money is no refund, my friend. Take it or leave it. Comprende?" Eddy said to him.

Los stared at him in disbelief.

Eddy asked him again, "comprende?"

And that was it. The straw that broke the camel's back. Los nodded his head, then put his hand in his pocket and pulled out the Gen 5 Glock 20 and put it in Eddy's face. Thank God for tinted windows!

"Now you muthafucking comprende!" Los growled at him. "I'm leaving with my money and these muthafucking pills! And you can let your brother know how you fucked up today." Then he grabbed the 10k from the center console and seen the gold-plated pistol and took that too. "Should've had this on your lap, my friend," Los told him, about to leave the car.

"You don't know how bad you just violated, holmes," Eddy said.

"I aint worried about it," Los said back to him.

SMACK! SMACK!

Then hit him twice in the face with his own gun, then grabbed the keys out of the ignition. "Be grateful yo brains aint all over the dashboard." Then he got out of the truck, leaving Eddy dazed and bleeding from his forehead and nose. He jumped back in the Beemer and got outta there.

The plug's brother. Damn. He met Bird in prison. They were both trustees on their unit; so they would chop it up all the time. Bird always boasted of his cartel ties and how he was getting deported on his release date back to Mexico and getting right back to the money.

They linked up after Bird snuck back into America. His dad died and him being the oldest son, the family business passed on into his hands. He had I-5 sewed up from California to Seattle. So naturally, Los needed a piece of the Portland pie.

Well, that was then and this was now. He tried calling Bird a few times but got no answer. *Fuck it, we go to war with anybody*, he said out loud to himself then turned up *"Thug Shit"* by K.T Foreign as he got on the freeway, headed to the spot.

***

"So let me get this straight, holmes," Bird said to his brother. "He gets in the truck, pulled his cuete, pistol whips you, took your keys and left with the pills?"

"Sí, hermano," Eddy replied.

"Just like that? You told him you spoke for me? That all re-ups were through you now?" Bird asked.

"My brother. These city guys are ungrateful. No loyalty to the hands that feed them. Mi? Soy tu familia! I tell you the truth."

What Eddy didn't tell his brother was that he kept a paint can for himself, and that his greed and stupidity were going to be the actions that eventually brought his family down.

"I see," Bird said and brought his hands together like he was praying and looked at his younger brother. "It will be blood for blood."

"Hermano. Let me pull the trigger," Eddy asked.

"You pull the trigger?" Bird laughed. "And have him take your gun again? I'll take care of this. Now get the fuck outta here." As his brother left, he looked at him and shook his head. He felt no remorse or sympathy. Would have even less of a headache if Los had just killed him. He knew his brother was a liability, but Eduardo was family, and this was a family business.

***

"Damn, so you smacked him with the pole, but aint smoke him?" HP asked Los then passed him the Backwood.

"Yeah, foo," Los told him as he puffed on the wood. "I could've, and shit I probably should've. No cap, but I like to fuck with a nigga mind. Smashed that muthafucka nose, he finna be breathing funny and shit the rest of his life and every time he look in the mirror and see that crooked muthafucka he gon' think 'bout me and have his head on a swivel. Spooked. 'Cause he know I'm outside and he's on my shit list."

"Shit, let's cross him off it then," HP said.

"I messaged his bro and told him to tap in with me. So 72 hours. If he don't tap in, I'm gon' take his absence of communication as what it is and we gon' score first."

HP looked at him, high as hell, and said, "I'm with it, brother." He looked at him some more and said, "Nigga, pass that shit."

They was at the homies' spot out in Clackamas, across the street from the mall. DG had an apartment there but the homies was there more than he was. Gang only. The ride-or-die Mafia niggas. Wasn't shit but 2 couches, TV on the wall and a PS5. A mattress on the floor in the bedroom, no box spring. Fridge empty as hell. But they was chilling though. If the walls had eyes they'd have seen everything but rape in that muthafucka. It got triv. The homies was ill.

Chapter 4

"Ugh, shit," Los said in his sleep. He opened up his eyes and saw Kaleah's mouth moving up and down on his dick. Instantly awake, he ran his fingers through her hair, gripping it—only motivating her to get on demon time.

When he was close to bussing, he pulled her head up, got up, and moved behind her. She arched her back, and he slapped her on the ass and pulled her head back by her ponytail.

"Who's pussy is this?" Los asked her as he rubbed his meat up and down her pussy lips.

"Yours, daddy," she moaned back.

"Bitch! I said who's fucking pussy is this?" he said to her again and slapped her ass cheek harder this time.

"Oooh, daddy! It's yours! All yours! Fuck me, please!" she begged him.

He slid in her and started stroking' her slowly, getting' his rhythm. He leaned over her body and started talking' that nasty shit in her ear that made her go crazy. He bit down softly on her neck, then stood up behind her and started drilling' her. She was arching her back and throwing' it back at him like a real bitch!

"Oooh baby I'm bout to cum!" she screamed out.

"Cum for me, baby," he told her.

"Oh shit, daddy! I'm cumming! Oh my God! I love you!"

Feeling her nut all over his dick, Los sped up and said, *"Damn, bitch, I'm bout to bust!"*

She squeezed her pussy on his dick. *"Cum in me, baby! I love you so much!"*

"AAAGGHH!" he grunted and shot his nut deep inside her. He rested his body on her back and stayed inside of her while he caught his breath. Then he pulled out and watched his nut drip out of her.

She flipped over, smiled at him, and said, "Good morning, babe."

"Morning. I'm finna hop in the shower. What you got going today?" Los asked her.

"Just a nail appointment. I'm off today," she responded.

"Bet," he said and walked to his phone and Cash App'd her $200 for her nails. "Let's go to Lincoln City today. Get a room on the beach. Hit the casino."

"I'm down, babe. I'll be back in a couple hours."

He hopped in the shower, and she got dressed. As she was almost out the front door, she remembered her tire was flat. She turned around, grabbed his keys off the kitchen island, and left.

After she got in his car, she looked around for condom wrappers, panties—anything scandalous. She was on it. Satisfied he wasn't doing nothing extra, she moved the seat up and left for her nail appointment.

Unknown to her, the La Familia Cartel gave that car description and areas to look for it to all their soldiers and everyone else they supplied in the Portland area.

Kaleah drove down Halsey Street on FaceTime with her mother. Los stayed on her about being aware of her surroundings, but she was so into the conversation she was slipping'.

Unaware of the van following' her for the last two miles, she stopped at the light on 122nd and Halsey.

The van pulled up next to her. Out of the corner of her eye, she saw the door slide open and the barrel of the chop. She stepped on the gas as it slid all the way open and the paisa started shooting'.

BRAAAAT! BRAAAAT! BRAAAAT! BRAAAAT!

He blew out the left back window and shot holes through the car. The van was no match for the German engineering, but he kept shooting'.

BRAAAAT! BRAAAAT! BRAAAAT! BRAAAAT! BRAAAAT!

Stepping on the gas when she did saved her life. They were never able to get right up on her. The bad angle, sloppy driving', and horrible aim had him missing' the car more than he hit it.

The van hit a side street once the sirens got closer. Her adrenaline was so high that she didn't realize she was shot 'til she looked down and saw the blood on her arm and the collar of her shirt. Then she felt it running down her neck.

Her mom was still on FaceTime screaming, a witness to the shooting. Kaleah looked at the phone and said, *"Mommy, I'm shot."* Then everything went black...

***

Los got the call from her mom and listened to her explain the situation in hysteria. He went to grab the keys from the kitchen and seen hers there and his gone. Then it all clicked for him. Bird struck first.

He got to the parking lot and seen her tire was flat. "Fuck!" he yelled. Then said, "Fuck it," started the car and rode 3 tires and a rim from 165th and Halsey to Adventist Hospital by Mall 205.

He pulled up to the emergency room entrance and parked. He got out and seen the rim was cracked in so many places it was through.

He walked in and went straight to the desk. "What room is Kaleah Bay in?" he asked.

"Let me look," the nurse told him. "She's in surgery right now. If you take the elevator to the 5th floor, there's a waiting room closer to her there."

"Thank you," he said and made his way to the elevator.

As he sat in the waiting room, her family started to show up. He hugged her mom, aunt, and sister. Then sat alone by the window. He didn't want anybody around him while he plotted murder.

Her mom walked over and sat down across from him. Even though she was a professional and highly respected in her career, she came up in the trenches and knew shit got ugly behind the scenes.

She looked Los in the eyes and asked, "How you doing, baby?"

"I'm fucked up. I love that girl to death," he told her.

"I know you do. We all do. Now I don't expect you to tell me why this happened, but I expect you to make this right. Understand me?"

He looked her in the eyes and seen the pain, anger, and hate that he felt—and knew they were on the same page.

"Aint no question, Mom," he responded.

Then the doctor came out.

"The family of Kaleah Bay?" he announced.

"Over here," her mother said.

"You're the mother?" he asked.

She nodded anxiously.

"Your daughter was very fortunate. She was hit by a large bullet. A 7.62. Luckily, it went straight through her shoulder—didn't even touch the bone. The other injury could've been way worse. She was grazed on her neck. The bullet took the skin off her tattoo. But that's it. We stitched her up and gave her 4 pints of blood."

"When can we see her?" Los asked him.

"She's sleeping right now. She can have one overnight visitor. The rest may come back during tomorrow's visiting hours."

They all looked at each other. Then her mother spoke up and told Los, "You should stay with her. She'll be happy to see you when she wakes up. You let me know when my baby wakes up. You hear me?"

He nodded his head. "Thank you," he said back to her, then left toward her room.

As he lay there watching her sleep, looking at the wires connected to her body, he vowed revenge. And after deep contemplation, he knew just what he was going to do.

By the time the sun rose, he still hadn't slept. He was laying down with his eyes closed and head resting on the arm of the couch in her room when he heard, *"Babe, get me some water."*

He opened his eyes at the sound of her voice, rushed to her, and put the straw in her mouth so she could drink from the glass. He put the cup down, and she said, "We still going to Lincoln City, babe?"

"Yeah baby. Just get outta here first. Tell me what happened though, Lee."

She told him everything, then cried about crashing his car. He told her he cracked her rim getting there, so they were even.

He called her mom and let her know she was awake and well. Once her family got there, he kissed her goodbye and left. It was demon time.

Chapter 5

Los and HP sat in the stolen Impala, parked in the corner of The Venue strip club parking lot on 99th and Stark. It used to be called The Mystic. Different name, same washed-up bitches. With a clear view of the entrance, they waited for this Mexican bitch Mona to come out.

Earlier in the day, he went to the strip club's Instagram page and seen on their story she was working 'til it closed tonight. They planned to snatch her up afterwards.

Los hit a fat key of powder, then passed the sack to HP, who did the same. "The bitch coming out right now, Blood," HP said to Los.

Los looked up and seen her. "The bitch kinda thick, huh gang."

"On God," HP said. "Start this janky shit up though. Let's get on this bitch."

And that's why Los had nothing but love and loyalty for him. It wasn't even his bitch that got popped, but he was ready to get jiggy for her. They lived by the motto "Any friend of mine, we gon' share the same enemies."

She pulled out, they followed her. Thirty minutes later, they were in North Portland, driving through the Columbia Villa.

"Damn, where this bitch stay, Blood?" HP said. "Just pull up next to her and blow her shit."

"Nah. That looks too random. I want her people to know who did this shit and why it happened. Set the demo with this," Los responded and kept following from a distance.

HP looked over and seen a demon behind the wheel and knew it was about to get ugly for whoever this thick bitch was. Fuck it, he thought, then hit the sack and passed it to his homie.

They drove down Fessenden and took a left on Wall Street and drove a few more blocks. "She pulling in to that driveway right there," HP said.

Los slowed down and parked on the corner. He looked in the backseat, seen a DoorDash bag, and got an idea. He grabbed it, grabbed his backpack, pulled his skeezy down his face, and got out the car.

They got to the porch and he put his ear to the door and listened. He heard her cussing some nigga out in Spanish over the phone and hanging up, so he knew she was alone.

He knocked on the door and said, "DoorDash," then held the bag up. She opened the door, and before she could say anything, he had his gun in her face, pushing her back into the house. HP ran in behind him and closed the door. Los pistol-whipped her, knocking her to the floor.

"Who are you? Why are you doing this?" she cried out through broken teeth.

He pulled his ski mask up and said, "Bitch, you know exactly who I am!"

All the blood drained from her face. "I have nothing to do with my uncle's business! I'm a female!" she pleaded with him.

"Bitch, that's exactly why I'm here," Los said. "Bro, tape this bitch mouth up. I'ma grab a chair so we can tie her up."

As he walked to the kitchen, he heard her tryna struggle, then a loud ass *SMACK!* Then nothing at all. He walked back to the living room with the chair and seen her sprawled out. "Damn nigga. I aint say knock the bitch out." Los laughed.

HP looked at him and raised his hands in the air, palms up. "The bitch tried to bite my finger off."

"Come on, let's get this bitch tied up," Los told him.

A few minutes later, and she was fully secured to the chair. He threw a cup of cold water in her face, waking her up.

"Nah bitch. It wasn't a dream. We really here. Now I'ma ask you some questions. It's going to get real painful around here if you lie to me. You understand me?"

She nodded yes.

"How much money you got in here? And before you lie, remember what I said about the pain 30 seconds ago."

"About 30 bands. Plus what's in my purse. Moneys in the kitchen under the sink in the detergent boxes."

"Oh you a clever bitch, huh?" Los said, then told HP to go grab it. He came back and threw it in the DoorDash bag, then flipped her purse for the rest of her twos and fews.

"Please just take it and go! I won't say anything! I swear to God, Los!" she cried out.

"See bitch, the thing about God is, he forgives. I don't. Where's your uncles at?" Los said to her. This question was just a formality. He had his mind made up in the hospital about the motive of this mission. The money was just a plus. This was about revenge. Nothing more, nothing less.

He didn't have to know where her uncles were at. This action would bring them out.

"I don't know! I haven't seen either of them! Please! You gotta believe me!" she pleaded with him.

Los didn't say anything back to her. He pulled the nail gun from his backpack that he had a smoker steal from Home Depot that afternoon.

"Damn nigga, that's vicious!" HP said, looking at the nail gun. "Them muthafucking nails long as hell."

Los looked at him, then looked at Mona, who just pissed herself in the chair, sweating bullets. "No no no noooo," she begged.

He shot her in the legs, stomach, chest. Six-inch nails embedded themselves into her body.

POP! POP! POP! POP! POP! POP! POP! That bitch was in the chair doing the Harlem Shake how them nails was hitting her chest!

Then Los pulled out a throwaway Taurus PT24 9mm and shot her three times in the face. No open casket. Wars got ugly. He took a picture of her, put the nail gun in his backpack, grabbed the DoorDash bag, and they ran back to the Impala.

Chapter 6

Eddy was laughing as he drove away from getting over on another of his brother's clients. He stopped at a red light, and there was a car in front of him. He felt on top of the world as he looked down at his phone screen to sniff the line of coke he had on it. He heard a car honk their horn and assumed it was the car behind him telling him to go. Without looking up, he stepped on the gas.

CRASH!

He smacked the car in front of him! He saw the paint can with the pills inside fly off the passenger seat, and the lid came off as it hit the floor. The sounds he heard next made him freeze and forget about everything else.

BLURP! BLURP!

Across the intersection, two motorcycle cops watched him rear-end the car. They pulled up faster than he could react and were telling him to step out of the car. They saw his wild, panicked eyes and the coke on his nose. He was cuffed and placed in the back of a responding police car on suspicion of D.U.I.

Upon searching his vehicle, they found $20K in cash, ten thousand fetty pills, and a loaded .45. The officer made a call and drove Eddy to the North Precinct.

***

The first four hours felt like twenty-four hours while Eddy was cuffed to the wall. He yelled and yelled, but nobody came for him. *Pinche putos. Probably looking at me right now behind that mirror,* he said under his breath, then flipped the mirror off.

2 HOURS LATER

Eddy looked up as the door opened and saw a man and woman walk in. The man spoke first.

"Eduardo, Eduardo. My brothers in blue told me you've been enjoying yourself in here."

Eddy grunted.

They sat down across the table in front of him.

"Anyway, I'm Special Agent Malone, and this is Special Agent Lopez," he said and pointed to the woman.

"I want my la—" Eddy was saying before Malone cut him off mid-sentence.

"Ah ah ah ah, before you finish that sentence and leave here directly to booking with a no-bail hold, you might wanna listen to what we have to say."

Eddy remained silent, suspicious of any deal the FBI might have for him.

"Thought you'd see it our way," Malone said. "So, looks like they recovered a lot of cash, a lot of fentanyl, and a firearm. The quantity of the pills alone is going to have you an old man on your parole date. Add to that your family's business and your ties to Mexico, you won't be granted pre-trial release either."

Eddy continued to eye them silently.

"Eduardo. We're your only ticket out of this mess. Your only ticket, my friend..." Malone told him.

"I'm no fucking rat," Eddy spat.

"You also don't look like a man that wants to spend the rest of his natural life in prison either. That's if you live to make it to trial. We're aware your brother is the one running the show. You don't play much of a part. You know what we're also aware of? You're viewed as the weak link, Eduardo. So what do you think your paranoid gangster brother is going to do when he finds out you've been arrested? I think he's going to eliminate a liability and not risk you bringing a RICO charge to the organization. In other words, you're dead, amigo."

Eddy felt himself starting to sweat. He knew Bird would have him killed just for having this conversation, so he spoke up.

"And what is it you want me to do?"

Agent Malone smiled. "So glad you asked. For starters—who killed Mona Hernandez, and why?"

My dead sister's only child, Eddy said and shook his head. *She was murdered by a punk puto named Los. He sent us a picture of her body saying "play ball."*

Agent Lopez was taking notes while they spoke.

"Los, huh? And what was the reason for this? I seen the crime scene photos—not pretty," Agent Malone said and shook his head.

My brother ordered a hit on him. Instead of killing him, a mistake was made and his lady was shot instead. She was driving his car and the shooters couldn't see behind the tint. She survived though.

Up to this point, Agent Lopez had just observed and taken notes; she hadn't spoken—till now.

"She was shot five days ago? Correct? Crashed and the shooters got away?" she asked.

"Yes, that's the one," Eddy said.

"You're familiar with this incident?" Malone asked her. She nodded her head yes.

"We're gonna cut you loose. I want you to find out the next cocaine and fentanyl import date. And don't think about running," Malone told him. "We're better at this than you."

They left the room and told the officers to release him in a few hours. *Make him sweat a lil more.* Malone noticed Lopez's silence but didn't address it 'til they got to the car.

"So, what do you think of our boy Eduardo?" he asked her.

"I think he's a piece of shit," she answered.

Malone laughed. "Naturally, he's that. So what's up with the girl who was shot and survived? How do you know her?"

"We went to high school together back home in Sacramento. Same group of friends. Lost contact when I left for college," Lopez answered.

"Seems like this Los character has her knee-deep in a dangerous game. Would you be able to use your connection with her to get close to him?" Malone looked at her and asked.

"The job comes first, sir," she said back to him.

"Great. Make contact and go from there. I trust your judgment." Malone turned the car on after her answer and headed back to the office.

***

"Babe, this place is nice, but I wanna be in my own bed, in my own home." Kaleah pouted to her man.

Los picked her up from the hospital and took her straight across the bridge to an Airbnb in Vancouver. He used an identity not connected to him or her to book it so they could stay off the map.

"Them fucking cartel niggas followed you from there. You must've took another Perc when I wasn't looking if you think you going back there any time soon," Los told her." So, get comfortable, put ya feet up an' shit. Call yo mom, sis, whoever to come keep you company. But too many people knowing your location defeats the purpose of you being here. So, keep this shit low key."

"Oh my God. Fine. It's whatever. So, you're leaving then? Already?" Kaleah asked him with an attitude in her voice.

"Damn, bitch, you got an attitude because I'm tryna keep you safe? I'ma hit you when I'm on the way back. Take this though." He handed her a black and chrome .380.

"A gun? Fo'real, babe?" she said.

“Yeah, a gun. It’s one up top, so keep the safety on. Flick this switch if it gets tricky while I’m gone. Red means dead,” he told her, then kissed her on the forehead and left. “Come lock this door though! And get some rest!” he yelled to her as he was leaving.

***

Kaleah layer in bed watching *Criminal Minds* and scrolling through her Instagram feed.

DING!

Someone DM’d her.

KL2020: Omg Lee! I miss you!

LeahBae: Kayla! How’ve you been?

KL2020: Good! Just moved back to the West Coast! Wbu?

LeahBae: Good! Ur back in Cali?

KL2020: No girl. I live in PDX. Fresh start. Looking for clients.

LeahBae: I live in PDX too! Clients?

KL2020: I’m a live-in caregiver /Physical therapist.

LeahBae: OMG! I need u! I’ll hire u RN! Come over!

KL2020: Wow! But k! Send addy N I’ll be omw!

Kaleah sent the location and called Los. He didn’t answer. She left a voicemail. “Babe! My friend is coming over. And she’s a fucking physical therapist! Imagine that. We’re gonna hire her. Call me back! I love you!”

Chapter 7

Los pulled up to the spot in Clackamas and parked the rental car he was driving. Kapone, HP, and Paris were already there.

"What's good with my killas?" Los said as he walked in and shook everybody up.

"How sis doing?" Paris asked him.

"She good, P. My bitch got hit with a chop and walked it off. She harder than a lot of these niggas," Los answered proudly.

"Sis a real one," HP said. "I got the drop on the candlelight. It's in an hour at Kenton Park."

"We finna crash that shit," Kapone said, excited to slide with the gang. He was mainly in Vegas doing his thang, so it wasn't every day he got to bond with his niggas through warfare.

"Y'all niggas ready?" Los asked the room, looking each person in the eye, seeing no hesitation in any of them.

Kapone answered for everybody by opening the hallway closet and passing out a Baby AR-15, a Baby AR-10, and two Drakos. They were out the door two minutes later.

***

Los pulled up and into the 24-Hour Fitness parking garage on 42nd. HP and Paris hopped out, and 30 seconds later were both behind the wheel of a stolen car. They followed Los out and pushed towards the candlelight.

Once they got close, they stopped a few blocks away. Los parked the rental, hopped out, and got in the stoley with Paris. Kapone did the same with HP. Both cars pulled up to the park. All four bounced out ready to drill shit.

Los seen a black SUV with two big Mexicans sitting in it that he assumed were bodyguards. An assumption was good enough for him. It was too late to clarify anything. He jumped onto the hood of the car and sprayed the windshield.

BRAAAAT! BRAAAAT! BRAAAAT! BRAAAAT!

Killed them instantly.

He heard his homies serving shit, so he turned towards the park, started red dotting any male he saw, and got jiggy!

THRAAT! THRAATATAT! THRAAT! THRAATATAT!

All hell had broken loose at Mona's candlelight service. Bitches was grabbing kids, huddling over them, protecting them with their bodies while their husbands, boyfriends, cousins, and uncles all got shot at. Unfortunately, a few bitches got they shit pushed back too. Casualties of war.

Los heard sirens, turned around, and seen the boys pulling up to the scene. He jumped onto the roof of the SUV he was standing on and started spraying them too!

BRAAAAT! BRAAAAT! BRAAAAT! BRAAAAT!

"Fuck the police!" he yelled and kept shooting into their patrol car. The windshield was covered with holes and blood.

"Come on! Let's get the fuck outta here!" he yelled to his homies and started shooting into the park, giving them cover and time to get to the getaway car. He jumped off the truck onto the road after they passed him and got into the driver's seat. He stepped on the gas, leaving the other stolen car in the middle of the street to block the road and anybody that might make the mistake of trying to follow them.

The surviving men in the park seen them leaving, so they started shooting at the car. Kapone stuck his Baby A out the window and ate their food one more time.

They pulled up to the rental car parked a few blocks away, got in, and left the stoley there and smashed to Columbia

Blvd. They made it to the freeway without a second look from the many police cars they saw speeding in the opposite direction, responding to the shooting.

Los cracked the roof and sparked a port. His hand was shaking from the adrenaline flowing through his body. “When you beefing with the cartel, you gotta do cartel-type shit. Nobody is safe,” he said.

“I don’t think the town ever seen some shit like that before,” Kapone said out loud to nobody in particular.

“I dropped at least five niggas back there!” HP said and laughed. “I’m gon’ see this through to the end with you, brother!”

“We gotta hit ’em hard like this every single time, my niggas. Stick and move,” Paris told them.

“And we gon’ hit ’em where it hurts every single muthafucking time,” Los said. He dropped them off in Clackamas, then went and dropped the Baby A’s and Drakos off to his white homie, Kobe. He had a 3D printer and would have the barrels, firing pins, and stocks replaced on all four rifles and back to him by tomorrow. No trace, no case.

***

Agent Malone pulled up to the crime scene at Kenton Park solo. As he got out of his car, he was met at the door by the head of the Portland Gang Task Unit—a bald Irish cop named Borlee. To say Borlee toed the line between crooked and righteous was an understatement. Since his wife left him, his only passion was the job: to lock muthafuckas up. By any means necessary. And if he had to get a lil crooked to accomplish this, it was all righteous with him.

“Special Agent Malone, FBI,” Malone introduced himself. “I assume you have the crime scene contained?” he questioned Borlee.

Is this asshole in a suit questioning my competence? Borlee thought to himself but said, “27 injured, 17 dead. Two of them children and two dead men in a truck. I got two dead officers, and I got dead fucking Mexicans everywhere. And these aren't Cortez and Dickie Mexicans. These are big truck, big belt buckle, big hat, and snakeskin cowboy boot Mexicans. What the fuck is going on here, pal?" Borlee asked heatedly.

Agent Malone took in the destruction around him and processed the scene in his mind. His roaming eyes stopped at a house with a direct view of the park and crime scene. He turned around as his mobile crime lab crew pulled up. He turned back to Borlee. "Containment looks great. You did good here, officer. But this is an FBI scene now. You and your men may leave after you've debriefed and turned over any evidence already collected to our techs," he said this as more of a demand than a professional request.

After dismissing them and getting his crime scene people up to speed, he walked to the house with the unobstructed view. He saw a Ring doorbell camera and smiled. *I'm on your ass now, motherfucker.*

***

Borlee sat in his car, pissed that the punk-ass FBI hijacked his case. He knew it had to be the same group that brutally killed Mona Hernandez that most likely came to her memorial to cause more death. And the suddenness of the big FBI presence hours later let him know there was more going on here than just a shooting—as horrible as it was. But fuck the FBI. This was his backyard, and he was gonna get to the bottom of this. One way or another.

***

Los walked into the house with his Gman out after seeing the strange car in the driveway. He didn't see anyone in the living room after he quietly let himself in, but he heard the TV on in the master bedroom down the hallway.

He got to the door and eased in, ready to shoot. "Oh my God! Babe, put that away. This is my friend Kayla. I left you a voicemail about her coming over," Kaleah told him.

Los looked at the female sitting in the bed next to his and saw a petite, Spanish girl with dark features, wearing leggings that fit like skin and a tight shirt with no bra underneath. Nipples poking. Bad bitch foreal. But next to Kaleah, she was average.

"Hey, I'm Kayla. Me and LeeLee go way back. I'm going to be helping her with her recovery. So we'll be seeing a lot of each other. Los, right? I feel like I already know you from how much she's said about you," she said and smirked, sticking her hand out for him to shake.

Before he could shake her hand or properly introduce himself, *"Breaking news"* popped up on the TV screen.

"Hi, this is Bonnie Silkman with Fox 12 News. We're here with breaking news out of Kenton Park in North Portland tonight, where officers say 17 people died and 27 more were injured, including two women and a pair of twin children. The first patrol car responding to the call was fired upon, killing the two officers inside. The shooters were masked and..."

"That is so fucking sad," Kaleah said as she watched the news segment.

"Sheesh. Them niggas wasn't playing," Los said and left the room.

Kayla told Kaleah she would be back in the morning. On her way to the door, she observed Los sitting on the couch, gun next to him. Still in his black Nike Tech sweat suit. She said goodbye and left to go summarize everything she saw and heard in her report when she got home.

Chapter 8

"This is unacceptable!" Bird yelled. He barely had shown up to the candlelight before the shooting started. He left his bodyguards in the car and entered the park alone. He watched Los gun them down and was powerless to prevent it. He returned to Mexico that same night.

The violent events taking place in Portland had made it hot for everybody. The news named the shooting at Kenton Park the *Memorial Massacre*.

As the boss of La Familia, he couldn't afford to slip up and find himself in booking or a grave. He reluctantly left Eddy in charge while he called the shots from Nayarit, Sinaloa.

He had men staking out Los' and Kaleah's apartments and hired a hacker to monitor debit card use and also to try to triangulate their phones using different places' cell phone towers to get their locations. So far, none of it was productive.

The money doesn't wait for no man, so it had to be business as usual. He rerouted the Portland shipment to a different warehouse to be on the safe side.

After a full day of quarterbacking from Mexico, he checked his phone for any updates. Still no word on his old partner's whereabouts.

***

RING! RING!

Los looked down at his phone and didn't recognize the number. He declined it. Ten seconds later, it rang again. Fuck it.

He quietly got out of bed and answered it when he was two steps out of the bedroom. “Who’s this?”

“Oh my fucking God! Papi, did you block me?” the caller asked him.

Maria’s faggot ass. He looked at Kaleah in a deep Perc sleep and continued down the hallway. “Bitch, it’s 8AM. What the fuck you want?” he asked her.

“Papi. This kitty misses you.”

“Bitch, bye.” Los started to press end.

“Wait! Wait! Wait!” Maria yelled. “My prima is going to visit her man at Sheridan today. Can you hook her up with some pills?”

“I aint hooking her up with’ shit. I’ll fasho sell her some though. Where she at? How many this bitch want?” Los asked her, thinking how he was finna tax this bitch Maria’s relative.

“Papi! You’re on speaker! But she’s here. And 500 if you have them.”

Do I have them, he thought and shook his head at her stupid-ass question. “$2500.” He told her the price.

“Mi amor. Let her pay $2000.” Maria tried to negotiate.

“Bitch, if she aint got it, you better loan her $500 or she getting 400 pills. I’m on the way.” He said and hung up without hearing her reply.

He entered the room and dressed quietly. When he was ready to go, he woke Kaleah up. “Babe, when that caregiving bitch getting here? Or text yo’ sis to pull up. I’m finna go buss a few plays, and you don’t need to be alone like that.” he caringly told her.

“K, babe. Be safe. I love you.” she said back to him, half asleep.

“I love you more.” Los told her, then leaned over her and kissed her on the lips, then left.

***

"I be paranoid, you blow yo' nose I might blow this Choppa. Niggas aint gang, aint FruitRidge if you aint know, poppa. I was starting 5 shooting guard on that old roster…"

Bris was talking the shit that Los was truly living, so he felt this song in his soul.

Los was a foreign or its boring type nigga fasho, but he was fucking with this Kia rental he was pushing from Hertz. He got off the freeway on Glisan and took a left, going towards 162nd... The numbers.

He wasn't worried about a nigga getting on him. The Kia was lowkey as fuck, plus that joint had 5% tints. Still though, he kept his pole on his lap and his eyes constantly scanned his surrounding environment for threats.

He pulled into the blue apartments on 162nd and Glisan, right before the corner store. He was getting out the car and seen a nigga coming down the same stairs that he was getting ready to walk up.

Did she line me up? were the first thoughts to cross his mind 'til the nigga came into his view. Then he quickly dismissed the idea.

Ace Boogie, an Alberta Park Mobb nigga. He hadn't seen him since he left the Mobb and started MAFIA. They locked eyes.

"What's up nigga? What time you on?" Los immediately asked him.

"Bitch, if you don't stop clutching that fucking gun," Ace said and closed the distance between them, embracing Los with a brotherly hug.

These niggas was Day Ones, and had did enough dirt together to get thrown under the prison. But Los was Mobb-k now and didn't know where Boogie stood.

"It's good to see you, brother. No cap. You went yo' own way for yo' own reasons. I aint mad at it." Ace Boogie said.

Los felt instant relief. The last thing he wanted to do today was leave his bro stanking in this parking lot.

"One hunnid," Los said, and they shook each other up with the B. "Just keep the same energy by yo'self or 100 deep, foo. Niggas be switching up."

"Aint no question." Boogie agreed with him. "Yo' niece and nephew miss you though. Pull up."

Man, I aint seen my dawgz in a minute, huh? You got the same line?" Los asked him.

"Same line, brother. Hit me."

"Bet that. I gotta chop it up with' you anyway. Shit been heavy. You strapped?" Los inquired.

"You knoooooow it." Boogie said, drawing out the word and patted his waistline.

"Bitch, you probably toting a Hi-Point." Los said and laughed.

"Nah, bitch. This FN 57'll leave holes in a sucka." Boogie told him, then pulled out a chrome gun with banana clip.

"Yeah, that's him my boy. Keep it on you, bro. I'ma tap in with' you later on." Los said and turned towards the stairs.

"Yup. Stay safe, brother." Boogie told him.

"Nah, brother. Them niggas better stay safe. Kuz I'm staying dangerous." Los said and walked up the stairs.

***

Maria opened the door before he could knock. "Why you doing ghetto shit in my parking lot?" she asked him with an attitude.

"Get some business, bitch," Los said and walked past her into the apartment. "Where yo' cousin at? She got the loaf or nah?"

Maria smacked her lips and closed the door. "Ask her," she told him and sat her sexy ass on the couch.

Maria was wearing red booty shorts that showed the bottoms of them lovely ass cheeks and a tight belly shirt. He looked around the living room; Maria was living nice these days. 100-inch Samsung smart TV on the wall, expensive black leather sectional couch, and candles burning on the coffee table. The aesthetic of the room had him respecting her a little more. Just a lil' though.

As he opened his mouth to ask where she was, she came out of the back room. What he saw was the baddest Latina bitch he ever laid eyes on. He was speechless for a few seconds as he took in her beauty, then remembered he was some game and got straight to business. Purse first, ass last was engrained in him since a younging from his trapping father.

"You the cousin, I assume." he said to her.

"You assume correct. I'm Dolce. Nice to finally meet you, Los." She stuck her hand out for him to shake. She looked at him with her big light brown eyes and held onto his hand longer than necessary.

This sexy bitch is dangerous, Los was thinking.

She let go and followed him into the kitchen. He was pulling the pills out when she pulled a stack of hundreds from her purse, counted out 25, handed it to him, then put the rest back in her Chanel bag. All blues.

Los peeped it and made a mental note to get her number before he left. "You a baller, huh?" he said to her.

"Nah. Just a grown woman... a focused grown woman." She spoke with a deep sexy Spanish accent that at any other time would have his dick deep down her throat already.

But not today. Today he was focused too. Plus, he didn't like to mix business with pleasure because bitches gon' start wanting fronts and free shit. He wasn't for it.

"I feel that." he said and put the money in his Gucci crossbody bag. "So, you on your way to Sheridan? Who you know up there?"

"My man. He's doing 20 years for guns and drugs. I wanna get these to him before they send him out of state."

Los looked at her and nodded his head in approval. Respect.

"I gotta be on my way though." she said and handed him her phone. "Here. Save your number. I'll hit you for more."

That accent again!

He saved his contact, then sent himself a text from her phone so he'd have her number too.

***

Maria was on her knees and elbows, positioned between Los' legs, making sure she licked every drop of nut that came out before she swallowed. Real bitch.

She looked up at him and smiled. She loved him deeply. She went to kiss him but was too slow.

He dodged her face and moved his body away. "Bitch. Watch out with' them sperm lips. The fuck." Los said to her.

She poked her bottom lip out and pouted, then went to rinse and brush them babies out of her mouth.

Maria had hella niggas checking for her and hella niggas tricking on her. But since she could remember, she had been stuck on Los. He was an asshole and rude as fuck. But you can't help who you love!

Every guy she talked to eventually got obsessed with her, and she would walk all over them. A turn-off.

Los though, he would treat a bad bitch like shit 'cause they were regular to him. He made a bitch shit on the pot or get off it!

She loved how nonchalant he was about her. How there was no question who was in charge when he was around. How every time he came around, he kept his foot on her neck. She loved chasing a man for once.

She knew about Kaleah, but she wasn't tripping. She would play her part like she was born for it.

Maria got back in the bed and laid her head on his chest. "I missed you, papi. So much. I love you and would do anything for you." she said to him.

"Oh yeah? Anything?" he asked her.

"Yes, baby. Anything. Just to have you with me."

"Straight up. So that's my pussy then, right?"

"Yesss. I'm yours completely." Maria answered and looked up at him. She would agree to anything just to be in his presence and have his attention.

"Shiiit. If that's my pussy, let's sell it then. You gon' bring papi a big bag!" Los told her.

He caught her off guard with that. That's not what she had in mind when she said she would do anything.

"Really babe?" she asked him.

"Dead ass, bitch. I do got something for you to do though," he told her, then got on his phone and airdropped her a photo. "His name is Eddy. I want y'all together in person ASAP. He's that dead bitch Mona's uncle. Bring her up if you have to. Just make it happen for me." Then Los proceeded to instruct her on the plan and what he wanted her to do and how to do it.

"I got you, mi corazón." she told him and continued to lay her head on his chest while he spoke.

***

"So I told her, 'Bitch I aint yo' baby dad! These is real diamonds!'" Paris was saying while they waited for the light to turn green on 122nd and Holgate.

DG cut him off. "Yeah, that's koo bro. But look across the street at the nigga standing next to the Buick with' the blond dreads. Who is that, G?"

Paris looked at the nigga loafing in front of the Plaid Pantry. "Shit, bro. That's Marky's bitch ass!"

"Say less, my boy. Park on the street. We finna bounce out on folks." DG told him.

The light turned green, Paris drove past the store, and parked on the next corner. They were out the load and in the parking lot five seconds later.

Marky was the big dawg in the Mobb and the main nigga stirring the pot and instigating on the sideline. Only on Facebook though.

He was a dangerous nigga ten years ago. But this wasn't ten years ago. Now all he played was defense, and the two niggas walking up on him were on offense pressing!

"What's up, Mobb?" DG yelled as he got closer.

"Nigga, fuck the Mobb!" Paris said right afterward.

Peeping the hostility, Marky went to draw down. But DG was faster.

"Uhn uhn, nigga. Don't reach, kuz I'll teach you something and leave you here! Peezy, take that nigga's heat!"

After being disarmed, Market went with a different strategy.

"Bro, what's this about? Y'all tripping right now," he said to them.

"We tripping, huh?" DG said, then smacked the shit out of Marky with the pole. "Nigga, we hella tripping! We the real Mack Q Gang! Long live my brother, nigga. Keep the saucy nigga's name out yo mouth!"

Marky looked up at him. "You got that, bro. You got that," he said.

"Nigga, I know I got that. Now get yo bitch ass up and strip!" DG told him.

"Come on, my nigga. You aint gotta do all that," Marky pleaded.

DG looked at Paris. "Peezy. He said we tripping. We aint gotta do all that. What you think?"

"I think this weak ass nigga better start taking clothes off," Paris said, and then upped Marky's own pole on him. "Nigga, you heard what the fuck I said!"

Marky reluctantly started taking his clothes off. He was down to his socks and briefs. DG took a picture to laugh at later.

"And give me yo phone and keys too. You walking home, G. Shit, you might catch a date out here, hoe ass nigga!"

They ran back to Paris' Benz truck and drove away, leaving Marky almost naked in the parking lot. He was humiliated and promised himself that he would kill them niggas.

Chapter 9

Caesar walked into the visiting room at Sheridan FCI with a fresh cut, Taylored khaki suit, and Space Jam Jordan 11's. He felt like the boss he knew he was.

He caught Dolce's eye and gave her a head nod. She got up and went to the women's bathroom. He sat down and took a sip of the cappuccino she purchased for him when she arrived and waited for her to come back out.

After a few moments, the guard at the desk headed in the direction of the visitors' bathroom. She came out, and he went in to secure Caesar's pack. This was the first drop. Caesar's case was high-profile; so everybody already knew what he was about before he got there. After a few conversations with an opportunistic guard, he had his CashApp and put him on the payroll.

"Mi amor," he greeted Dolce with a kiss and hug. "I got good news," he said to her after they sat back down.

"And what is that, baby?" she asked him.

He leaned in towards her so she could hear him speaking low. "My lawyer has uncovered the location of Manuel and Juan. Without their testimony I would've never got found guilty. If they disappear, I could come back on appeal and come home, my love," he told her, taking her hands in his as he spoke.

"That's wonderful news, baby! I'll let Johnny know when I leave here," Dolce replied.

"No... Don't tell my brother anything about what I just told you. Approach Los about it. Check his temperature. I've been hearing some interesting things about him. It seems we have a mutual enemy," Caesar said.

"Five minutes!" the guard at the desk announced.

"Next time, get here earlier, baby. And approach Los ASAP," Caesar told her.

"I got you, papi. I love you," Dolce said, then stood up, kissed him, and left. She walked out of the prison wondering about Caesar's decision to approach Los about the witnesses and the sudden decision to distance himself from his brother and what it all meant.

***

Caesar got back to the unit and celled in for count time. After count was cleared, he skipped chow and stayed on the unit to talk business in a more private setting than the chaotic yard.

His homeboy considered himself a thinker; so he preferred to conduct business over the chess board.

Caesar watched his opponent trap his queen and, two moves later, checkmate him. "Damn," Caesar said under his breath, then congratulated him on the win.

"Your game is improving. You had me on the ropes for a second," Cream told him, then threw a couple air jabs.

"Run it back?" Caesar asked.

"In a minute," Cream said. "I told you my bro is good business. He be coming through in the 4th quarter like Curry every time." Referring to Los.

"Yeah, my wife said everything was smooth. Good look on the introduction. I see a lot of money in our future. Especially if I can get the fuck outta here," Caesar said, thinking about the witnesses standing in the way of his freedom.

"Minor setbacks for major comebacks, homie. Bro's murder game is official. After shorty tap in 'bout them two roadblocks to your freedom, they not gon' be on this side of the earth too much longer. Trust me," Cream told him.

Caesar nodded his head. "Yo, I appreciate you, my boy. And we gon' do big things in that world. This a token of my appreciation right now though." Caesar said and tapped Cream's leg under the table and passed him a pack of 100 pills.

Cream tucked the pack in his waistline. "Good look, my nigga." He stood up and said, "I'm finna put this up and hop on the jack. We gon' run it back tonight."

"Aww. Now you ducking the chess fade? Come on, Brody!" Caesar said jokingly.

Cream laughed. "You still not ready, foo. You almost there though." He dapped Caesar up and left the table.

Caesar went to his cell and laid down. His thoughts eventually ran to Los and his possible pending freedom. If Los made that happen, he'd bring him into the organization. He asked Cream if he should offer his family's help in going against La Familia, but understood when Cream told him that Los wanted to do this with his own team. Plus, this was a test of sorts, and he wanted to see if Los had it in him to play in the big leagues. Caesar was impressed thus far.

***

"So nice of you to join us, Agent Lopez," Malone told her as she walked into the conference room. "Our buddy Eddy was just about to say when the next big shipment was arriving."

"Next Friday. I mean Saturday the 15th," Eddy told them.

"So that's eight days," Malone said.

"Yes," Eddy said, agreeing with him. He was nervous, sweating in the air-conditioned room.

"And where is this happening, Amigo?"

"North Portland. Warehouse next to the bridge," Eddy answered.

"That would be the St. Johns Bridge?" Lopez asked him.

"What other fucking brid—"

SMACK!

Agent Malone was on him before he could blink and slammed his head against the wall for his disrespect.

"Don't insult my partner, you Mexican piece of shit!" Malone looked at Lopez after the last part and said, "No offense, partner."

She nodded her head in appreciation and understanding.

"Aagghhh!" Eddy screamed out.

Malone had mushed his face as he was pushing his head into the wall, reinjuring Eddy's broken nose.

"Shut the fuck up, Eduardo. You see anyone in here with you but us? Exactly. Now fucking apologize for your outburst," Malone ordered him.

"Sorry," Eddy mumbled under his breath. It came out as "sawwy" due to the injury.

"As you were saying, Amigo?"

"The drugs are getting dropped off Friday night and picked up throughout the day and night Saturday," Eddy told them.

"On Saturday, be here. We're going to wire you up. Get some real evidence against your brother and put him in a cell, and put you in that top spot," Malone told him and patted him on the back. "Imagine that; a rat for a jefe. Now get the fuck outta here!"

After Eddy left, Malone sat Lopez down so she could debrief him. "So what's the latest?" he asked her.

"Other than an expensive lifestyle, I haven't seen much. He's barely there. And either she's an Oscar-worthy liar or she's truly naive to his bullshit," she told him.

"So no progress essentially," Malone said to her, which pissed her off.

Lopez took a deep breath, then answered, "Listen, I don't need your condescending bullshit today or your impatience! I'm damn near deep undercover at this point! So even meeting you like this is dangerous. I can't imagine the consequence if I was seen even in the same building as Eddy!" she said to him, raising her voice. "You know what I've learned? I've learned by observing him and looking into his eyes that he's a killer if you push him. And it seems that our buddy Eduardo and his brother have pushed him. So now he's pushing back." She finished and looked at him, daring him to question her work again.

"Well said. Keep up the good work. I'll see you Saturday the 15th to wire our boy up. Til then, be safe and keep your eyes open."

Chapter 10

"A fucking Chevy van, bro? My G-ma used to have one of them joints," Los said as he inhaled and blew clouds of the Runtz smoke out his nostrils. He passed the blunt back to Ace Boogie.

"Yeah, my boy. Got the shag rug in that joint. Second row seats spin, the back seat like a fucking couch!" Boogie said and started to cough after hitting the Backwood too hard.

"I see you still smoke like a bitch, brother," Los told him and took the wood back.

"Fuck you, nigga," Boogie said after catching his breath. "That's some gas! But anyway, I'm finna grab that muthafucka. $1200 on OfferUp."

"$1200? That shit finna break down 12 blocks from where you bought it."

"Nah, I'ma get a tune-up and shit gon' be good. Bro, so look; see how we in the load right now? Smoking and chilling? Nigga, in the Chevy van niggas can post up. Run the 2K, shit bring some hoes in that muthafucka! We lit!" Boogie exclaimed, dead ass.

"I feel it, bro. That's the tree talking though," Los said.

"The tree? No bitch, nigga, I been had this idea!" Boogie told him.

DING!

Los looked down at the phone and smiled.

"Ruth's Chris? 7 pm?"

He replied right away. *"Bet."*

Boogie seen him smile when he read the text. "This nigga think he got hoes," he said and started cracking up.

"Think? Nigga, you and I both know this! Shit, the bitches know this! And this one right here? This that top of the line fine wine Carlo Rossi!" Los shouted, quoting E-40.

"But anyway bro, back to the bitch ass nigga Eddy! I got the bitch on him right now. You already know Maria can smell a trick a mile away, so she gon' have some results for me ASAP," Los said to him.

"Man, that bitch got a nose like a muthafucking German Shepherd!" Boogie joked, and they both started laughing.

"Foreal, huh?" Los said, agreeing. "But anyway, you tryna rock when it's go time?" he asked.

"Yup. It's green, bro. I'm with it," Boogie answered.

"My nigga," Los said and dapped him up.

RUTH'S CHRIS
7:15 PM

"My bad. You know how parking be around this muthafucka," Los said after he arrived and walked up silently, sliding into the booth across from her in the back corner of the restaurant, facing the window and the door.

Dolce looked up from her phone and smiled at what she saw. Los was wearing a white Burberry tee with the plaid pocket, black ripped Purple Label jeans, and the Burberry trainers with the strap by the toe. When she smelled the Dior Sauvage cologne coming off his body, she felt her pussy getting soaked. She squeezed her legs together unconsciously and felt her pussy tingle. She felt herself get goosebumps on her skin.

Dolce had on a black Valentino sundress, red bottoms on her feet, and a Valentino clutch wallet. All eyes on them.

"Your tardiness is excused this time, sir," she replied playfully, looking at him over the rim of her drink.

"Just this time, huh?"

Dolce smiled at the way he said *"this time."* Like he already knew this was one of many nights out together.

"But anyways, next time we gon' arrive together," Los said, taking control of the conversation and waving the server over to their table. "Let me get a shot of 1942, the reposado. And a pineapple and 1942 on ice on the side. And bring her another one of those," he pointed to Dolce's wine glass.

The server left to fill their drink order.

"So how'd the visit go?" he asked her.

Dolce looked at him before she spoke and thought about how much she should or could trust him and felt the vibe his energy had produced once he sat down with her. She went with her gut.

"Great, thank you. I'm actually here to discuss that with you."

Then she broke it down to him. She told him about the 20-year sentence, the witnesses lying on the stand, and about the opportunity of Caesar's freedom if they no longer existed. Then she brought up the twenty thousand.

"Twenty bands for two bodies?" Los asked her.

"Yes. Payable upon completion," she answered.

"Shiiit. Say less. The last snitch nigga got smoked for free," Los said.

The server finally arrived with their drinks.

Los raised his shot and tapped it against her wine glass and made a toast. "To success. Wealth. Health. And happiness." Then knocked the shot back. "We locked in, baby!" He stared into her light brown eyes and got lost in them as he said that last part.

Dolce had to stop herself from almost not keeping it strictly business with this impressive young man. She opened up her clutch and pulled out a small burner phone. "We will communicate about this only on these," she said, referring to the burner phone in her hand and the one in her clutch. "Pictures and information on both targets are in the notes. My other number is already saved in the contacts," she told him and handed him the phone.

"Bet," Los said and took the phone. "I'ma hit you when the job is done. We gon' celebrate!" he told her and got up, went to the desk by the door, and pulled out a few hundreds. He pointed to Dolce. "Her dinner is on me tonight. The rest goes to the server as a tip." Then walked out.

As he strolled to his car, he thought about the financial avenues this could lead to. A millionaire has at least 7 streams of income. Depending on the outcome of this job, this could possibly be another for him: murder for hire.

A fucking hitman, he said out loud when he reached the car. He got inside and laughed at where life was taking him lately.

As long as the outcome is income! And with that thought, he got into traffic.

Chapter 11

Sergeant Borlee found Speedy leaving Dawson Park, walking by Williams Street Market, and pulled over. "Get in." He'd forgotten how bad the smoker smelled. "Jesus, Speedy." He cracked the window.

"What?" Speedy replied. He was anxious and sweating. He was doing bad and needed a sack ASAP to get well.

"You ever shower?" Borlee asked him.

"I don't got no shower," Speedy responded matter-of-factly.

"Get a bar of soap and jump in the Willamette then," Borlee said and cracked the sunroof. "You hear about the shooting at Kenton Park?"

"Yeah. Real bad shooting," Speedy said with his hands between his legs, rocking in the seat.

"Yeah. Real fucking bad. What have you heard about it?" Borlee asked.

"Me? Heard something about a mass murder? Not Speedy!" he exclaimed.

"Look, motherfucker. I can bust you for paraphernalia and keep you for 3 days on a county hold. You like detoxing next to a piece of shit that smells worse than you? Begging you for your fucking bologna sandwich?" Borlee threatened him.

"You a real cruel muthafucka, man," Speedy said to him, knowing how serious Borlee was.

"Cruel, rude, asshole. I've been called worse by better. Motherfucker, I'm the law. What you got for me?"

Borlee opened up the center console and unlocked a steel box he had welded there and pulled a dub sack of heroin out.

Speedy eyed the dope. His pulse quickened. His mouth got dry.

Borlee handed him the bag. "Get well. Then tell me everything you've heard on the street."

"In the car?" Speedy asked.

"This one time," Borlee said. "Hurry the fuck up."

Speedy opened the baggie and poured the dope into a spoon he pulled from the dope kit in his jacket pocket. He put the Bic flame to the bottom of the spoon and cooked the dope. He dropped a cotton ball in the spoon, put the syringe to it, and filtered the heroin through it, leaving the impurities behind in the cotton ball.

"That motherfucker clean?" Borlee asked, referring to the needle.

"Cleaner than your Irish nuts," Speedy said back to him, already in a pre-high trance. Speedy tied his arm off and searched for a vein. He found one by his wrist and shot up. He nodded off instantly.

SMACK!

Borlee slapped the silly smile off his face. "The party's over. Talk to me."

"You ever hear of Mafia?" Speedy said, rubbing his sore cheek.

"The Mafia? Like John Gotti? Get the fuck outta here," Borlee said to him.

"No, but they for damn sure on they way! Damn, Borlee. You the police! How you don't know about Mafia?"

Borlee gave him a look that said *stop playing with me*.

"Anyway. Them boys aint playing. My nephew's a member. High ranking," Speedy said proudly.

"Your sister's son? Lil Delon? If Delon's around, Los aint too far away. What are they into?"

"Everything. Listen man. The word is, the head nigga's bottom bitch got popped driving his car. So now he's taking it to the cartel! Not some gang calling themselves the Cartel either. But the real muthafuckas from Mexico!" Speedy informed him.

"Bunch of fancy dressing Mexicans?" Borlee asked.

"I mean, regular Mexican cowboy shit. But sure," Speedy replied. "You want the real 411 though, Sarge?"

"And what's that, Speedy?" Borlee asked him, knowing Speedy phrased it that way to get some more H from him. Borlee grabbed another bag and tossed it at him. "This better be good."

"Old man across the street from the park got the whole thing on his Ring camera!" Speedy said and pocketed the dope fast.

"Call me, Speedy, if you hear anything else. Now get the fuck out," Borlee told him. "Now I gotta switch this car out for a fresh one."

"Rude muthafucka," Speedy said and got out.

"Call me!" Borlee shouted at him then sped off on a mission.

***

Sergeant Borlee pulled up to the week-old crime scene and parked his car across the street. Noon on a summer day and the playground was empty. Mothers didn't want their children playing at the scene of so much blood and death. Even though it was a week old, blood still stained the concrete in many places.

He got out of the car and the hairs on his neck stood up. Death still lingered in the air. He shivered and shook it off.

He walked over to the bullet-riddled Tahoe and wondered why the city or better yet the FBI hadn't towed it yet, but it was part of an active investigation?

Incompetent motherfuckers, he thought, disgustedly.

He tried the door and to his surprise it opened right up.

"Jesus Christ."

After sitting in the sun for a week, the interior of the Tahoe smelled foul. There were pieces of brain matter, bone, and blood everywhere.

He pulled a handkerchief from his pocket and covered his nose while he looked around the car. He put his hand under the front passenger seat and felt around. He pulled out an iPhone.

"What do we have here?"

He tried the power button. Dead. He put the phone in his pocket and continued looking for anything the forensic team might've missed. Finding nothing else, he closed the door and texted his cousin the location to come tow the car to a lot he owned. After stripping the car of the VIN, replacing the windshield, and a thorough detail, the car would be right back on the street next week. And he'd be a few thousand richer.

He looked at the houses across from where the shooters got out of their cars and started shooting and wondered how he missed it the day he responded to the crime. A fucking Ring camera. He owed Speedy another sack at least.

He walked over to the house and rang the bell.

"Portland police. Open the door please. Just have a few follow-up questions."

BEEP!

"Put your badge to the camera please."

Borlee pulled his badge out and put it to the camera.

A half-minute later, an elderly man came to the door and invited him into his home.

"Sergeant Borlee," he said and extended his hand to the old man.

The old man looked at him the way only 70 years of experience gives you, as if he was weighing his character.

"Herman."

They shook hands.

"This shouldn't take long. A week ago there was a shooting at the park. I'm following up. Did you see anything unusual before or after that—"

Before he was able to finish his sentence, Herman interrupted. "You mean unusual like a mass murder?"

"Yes. I agree. That was highly unusual. I noticed you have a Ring doorbell camera. Did you catch the shooting on it?" Borlee asked.

Herman walked to the fireplace and picked up a card from the mantle and brought it to Borlee. "I spoke to Agent Malone with the FBI and gave him a copy of the footage."

"Well I'm doing my investigation independently of the feds. I'm head of the Gang Task Force unit and this happened in my backyard. My turf. So I'm personally invested in this matter. May I get a copy of the footage also?"

"Well, I suppose so," Herman said and pulled his phone out.

DING!

He airdropped the video to Borlee's phone.

"My grandbaby taught me how to do that," Herman said proudly.

Borlee smiled at how happy the old man looked when he brought up his grandchild. This caused Borlee to look around the living room, at the photos decorating the walls.

"Are you living here yourself, sir?" he asked Herman after noticing the home lacked a feminine touch.

"Yeah, just me. My daughter lives in Salem with her family. My boy died in Iraq. His mama died of a broken heart not too long after. But I'm holding on. I don't know what for. Just am." Herman told him, then looked him in the eye when he said the next part. "You catch these cock suckers, Sergeant. No courtroom justice either." And stuck out a gnarled old hand for him to shake.

Borlee took it and gave his word. "I wouldn't have it any other way, sir." Then handed him a card with his personal cell number on the back. “If you ever need anything, give me a call. Anything, sir.”

“Will do.” Herman took the card and opened the door for him.

***

Borlee sat in his car and thought about the old man living out his last years alone and wondered if his future held the same fate.

Gonna have to send him a hooker every now and then. He laughed at the thought.

He took out his phone, pulled up the footage and pressed play. The angle the camera had of the shooting was amazing. He couldn’t have asked for a better camera location without a GoPro. It caught the whole thing.

He watched as both cars pulled up and four people exited with automatic rifles. One of the shooters jumped onto the hood of the Tahoe and started firing into the windshield, overkilling the two people inside, while the other three ran into the park and started firing shots at the people running. Twenty seconds later, the shooter on the Tahoe turned his head and looked at something off camera. Then jumped from the hood to the roof and started shooting in that direction. He then jumped from the truck onto the street and started firing into the park while the other three got in the car. He then got in the driver’s seat and they drove off.

Borlee finished the video and replayed it slower, watching it again. He saw the shooter on the Tahoe wasn’t wearing gloves. This is the one he wants.

You can’t see on camera who he was shooting from the roof of the truck, but Borlee knows because he responded to the call. He shot Borlee’s brother officers. This was the cop killer. He paused the video and zoomed in. He could see tattoos on the shooter’s hands, but the quality of the video wasn’t good enough to make out the details of them.

With the info Speedy gave him earlier, he at least has a point to start from.

He flipped open the laptop on his passenger seat and typed in *Carlos Mills*. The shooter is too light to be Speedy's nephew. Carlos' profile popped up. He clicked on *Distinguishing Marks* and then on *Tattoos*. He saw that both his left and right hands had tattoos.

I got you now. Cop killing motherfucker.

Chapter 12

Flashback

"Kuddin, the news had yo mugshot next to a pic of the work like you was El Chapo!" Los said into the phone.

Cream laughed. "I know. America's worst nightmare. Shit look worse than it is though. My BM dropped 50 off to my lawyer a few days ago so we good. You know how this shit go though, family. Just gotta sit down and wait this shit out."

"I hear that. I got you too. Whatever you need. It's good," Los told him, meaning every word.

"I know you do. Look, I need you to go to my lawyer's office downtown and pick up this envelope I gave him for you. This shit gon' blow yo mind, P. After you read it, you gon' know what you need to do, you feel me?" Cream said to his younger relative, confident in his decision-making.

"Say less. I'ma head that way now," Los told him. "Keep yo head up, my nigga."

***

The paperwork Los had in his hand truly did blow his mind. And broke his heart. Turned it cold. The feds had kicked in his older cousin Cream's door and arrested him on drugs and an Armed Career Criminal charge. This wasn't just some random relative to Los though. When his parents died, his aunt and uncle took him in and raised him with their own son.

Los and Cream grew up as brothers and were close like that. They were only 2 years apart. This whole time they thought the opps had given him up to take him out the picture, on some hater shit. Not knowing it was a snake in their own grass that had bit them.

Their homeboy, like a brother to both of them, had got into a drunk car crash and the police found 5 bricks of raw cocaine in the trunk and a Glock 20 with an extended magazine in the glove box.

The feds got involved right away. Alleging that the gun was present to protect the drugs, they threatened him with 30 years in a USP. He folded instantly.

They gave him a narrative they wanted him to use and he set up one of his best friends. And to top it off, after they kicked in Cream's door and took him away, he went back the same night and pulled the floorboards up and stole 50k from him. A true snake nigga.

Cream's arrest broke their mother's heart. Los dropped tears while reading' the discovery. He knew what had to be done.

Their *homeboy* thought he was safe because the paperwork had a protective order on it, blocking' his information as the criminal informant. But the feds slipped like they always do.

He sent a text: *"We finna meet Cream's plug tonight. Wya?"*

"The bitch house. Where at?"

"Marine Drive. Meet me there in an hour."

"Bet."

In an hour, it would be dark. After he killed him, he could get rid of the gun and the body in the Columbia River.

Los pulled up half an hour before he was supposed to and sat in his car, looking at the water in deep thought. He hated what he was about to do. But he hated the reason why he had to do it even more. *Fucking snitch nigga.*

After everything they did for this nigga, this is how he repaid them. They helped get him on his feet. Helped him buy his first car. The nigga had never left Oregon 'til they took him on the road with them to LA and Vegas. He never had more than $500 before he met Los and Cream. They bossed him up and changed his life. Now Los had to end that same life he helped change.

He saw the blue Mustang pulling' up in his rearview. He cocked his gun, put it on his waistline, and got out the car.

Mack got out the Mustang and gave his homie a pound. "Nigga, take this shit to the car wash. Sheesh." He said jokingly and ran his finger along the roof of Los' AMG550, then wiped the imaginary dust off his fingers.

"Yeah right, nigga. You know my shit is immaculate," Los said back to him, playing along. "You think this nigga gon' fuck with us? And if so, are we going to get 'em same price bro was getting 'em for?" Mack asked him.

"I don't see why not. It aint like bro is dead. He just sitting down for a minute. To the plug, I'm an extension of him," Los answered as they walked down the marina. "I always wanted a boat. I'ma get me one next summer. On God. Something like that." Los pointed to one at the far end so he could lead him down there without suspicion.

"Yeah, that bitch is clean. Shiiit, I'ma get me one too then! We gon' be back-to-back! Boats and hoes, baby!" Mack said, walking ahead of him to get a better look at the sleek, luxury speedboat.

"I read the paperwork, bro," Los said to him. Mack spun and at the same time was drawing down. But Los was ready for him.

BLAKA! BLAKA! BLAKA! BLAKA!

Los' shots hit him in the chest and shoulder, causing Mack to fall. He started crawling, trying to get away. Los stood over him and kicked him in the ribs, flipping him over.

"Look at me, you bitch ass nigga!" Los yelled at him.

"Bro, don't kill me. Please." Mack begged for his life, spitting up blood with each word. *I'm yo brother*, he pleaded.

It fell on deaf ears.

My brother? Los spat, then shot him in the legs.

BLAKA! BLAKA! BLAKA!

"I thought you was my nigga," Mack said, staring up at him.

"Yeah? And I thought you was a real nigga. We was both wrong."

BLAKA! BLAKA! BLAKA!

He threw the gun into the river as far as he could. Then squatted next to Mack's lifeless body. He reached out and shut his eyes.

"You paid yo debt, brother. See you in the next life," Los said and dropped a tear for him, then pushed his body off the dock into the cold, murky water and watched it sink. Then went to the Mustang, retrieving the 50k from the trunk.

He grabbed an oil-soaked rag that was sitting next to the bag of money. He left the Mustang and put the bag in the Benz, then went back to the Mustang. He stuck the rag as far as it would go down the gas tank and lit the end on fire. He rushed back to the Benz and got in. He was leaving the parking lot when the car exploded.

Chapter 13

Los texted HP: *"Wya?"*

While he waited for a reply, he studied the pics and info Dolce had provided on the targets. *This is a thorough bitch*, he thought approvingly.

From what Los was reading about the soon-to-be-dead brothers, he was getting an idea about what her husband was into. At this point, murder was nothing to him; just a means to an end.

HP responded: *"the house."*

Los: *"Im finna slide."*

HP: *"Bet."*

***

It turned out that Maria's aunt used to date Eddy. She told Maria where to find him. That night Maria did her makeup, put on a skin-tight black dress and Valentino pumps. She had a French manicure (white tips) with the pedicure to match. Sexy ass bitch.

She checked herself one last time in the mirror, then double-checked her purse for the magnetized GPS unit Los gave her to leave in or on Eddy's truck. She hopped in her Audi and left.

She drove to 190th and Stark, parked in the same lot as the hood-famous taco truck. She redid her lipstick, got out the car and went into the Spanish dance club.

Confident that she was the baddest bitch in the building, she walked like it to the bar with all eyes on her. She ordered a Hennessy Lemon Drop. While she waited for her drink, she sent Los a text: *"at the club babe."*

Los: *"fsfs. Turn yo location on."*

Maria: *"just did. I'll lyk when he comes in."*

Los: *"Bet."*

She hearted the message and put her phone away. The club was packed with paisas looking to trick off! Any other time she would've been finessing a bag, but tonight she had a mission. An objective.

The lights were low and the dance floor was packed with couples dancing to the music being played by the live salsa band on stage.

She took a sip of her drink and looked around the club. She moved her eyes to the door at the same time Eddy was walking in with his entourage.

Eddy gave his drink order to one of his guys and he headed to the bar while Eddy made his way to the video poker machine.

Maria sent Los a text right away: *"making contact babe."*

Los: *"aight. Be smooth."*

Maria: *"always mi amor."*

She put her phone in her gray and white checkered Louis Vuitton bag, picked up her drink and made her way to where Eddy was already losing his money.

"God damn machine!" Eddy yelled as he lost another $100.

His security arrived with a bucket of Modelo for all of them just as Maria sat down at the machine next to him.

"Gracias, carnal," Eddy told his man and took a swig of the beer. He looked over at Maria and said, "Aye, Mami! *Mi gusta!*"

Maria smiled at the compliment and said, "Gracias, señor."

"No, thank you," Eddy told her. "And lose the señor, eh? I'm not so old." He flirted with her.

Maria put $20 in the machine and put on her acting skills. "I never know what game to play. I always lose my money."

"I can help you with that," Eddy said and pulled a knot of hundreds from his pocket and put $100 into her machine. "Always better to have more to play with, eh?" He continued his flirting and winked at her.

"More is definitely always better," Maria flirted back, thinking about the money Eddy just flashed and how she was going to bring it back to Los.

Eddy moved his seat closer to her machine and picked a game for her: Big City 5s, then pressed max bet and said, "The goal is get as many 5s on the screen as possible or in a row."

Maria pressed the button a few times while they continued to flirt and lost money every time she pressed down. Then *BOOM!* She hit the bonus. Five 5s in a row. $5500. Eddy laughed with joy. "Time to cash out, eh? Maybe you want a real bonus?"

Maria hit the cash-out button and took her ticket and put it in her bag. "But you just got here."

"Aahh! This is boring. Let's have some real fun," Eddy said and winked at her again.

"Well, I drove—" Maria was saying.

"That's fine! My guy can drive your car. You can ride in the truck with me," Eddy said, desperately trying to persuade her.

Maria didn't want to seem eager, so she said, "But sir, you don't even know my name. I could be a serial killer." She joked.

This stupid slut, playing hard to get, Eddy thought, but said, "What's the name to match the beautiful face? And I might have a serial killer fetish." He lamely joked. "Pero, lo siento for not asking sooner."

Maria laughed. "Apology accepted. My name is Yasmine."

"What a beautiful name! Yasmine. I love it. So are you ready to come keep me company?"

"Yes. Let's go," Maria said.

She handed Eddy her car keys and he passed them over to one of his security team. She finished her Henny Drop and got up to leave. Eddy took her hand in his and guided her to the exit. They got to the black Escalade EXT, he unlocked it and they both got in.

Maria sent a text to Los: *"With him. Going to his place RN."*

Los: *"be safe. Keep yo location on n don't forget to GPS the car!"*

Maria: *"I won't babe."*

As she sent that last text, Eddy looked at her and said, "Please, no more phones. I require all of your attention tonight, beautiful." Then took out the knot and peeled off ten hundreds and handed it to her. "This is just the beginning. *Mas para ti! Pero alrato!*"

Maria put the phone and money in her purse and settled in for the ride. Preparing herself to do what she had to do to get the job done tonight.

The things I do for love, she thought.

Los pulled up to HP's spot and parked. Before he got out the car, he checked Maria's location—still driving. He put his phone in his pocket and got out the car. He walked up the steps and knocked on the door.

To his surprise, Juice opened it and let him in.

"When you get back, bro?" Los asked him as he sat down and poured a shot of the 1942 sitting on the coffee table.

"Shit, just a lil bit ago. Heard my bros been going up with'out me." Juice said and poured a shot for himself. They tapped glasses and threw the shots back.

"To health, wealth, and happiness," Los said the toast.

"Straight up. So what's been going on? This nigga HP said it's been funky for the home team. That nigga upstairs by the way," Juice told him.

"Man, where do I start?" Los said and laughed. "Nigga, the body count been going up, brother! The home team been scoring. We finna press play on these niggas again real soon. Like a few days. You rocking?" Los asked him.

"Shit, you aint even gotta ask, Blood. You know I'm with' you. How we doing it?" Juice inquired.

"I got the bitch on ol' boy right now. We finna switch shifts and babysit this nigga 'til he lead us to the bag," Los answered him.

"Bet. Who all rocking?"

"Me, you, HP, and Boogie. Peezy and Kapone back in Vegas," Los said.

"Boogie?" Juice questioned.

"Yeah, bitch. Boogie. That's our brother. Day one nigga right there. I seen bro and chopped it up with' him. Aint no hard feelings. Shit, he might just join the team," Los said and poured another shot. "Regardless though, bro is rocking."

"It's good. Phoenix though? Wide open, my nigga. I'm finna get a spot out there. Bad bitches that love to pay a nigga. Plus it's hours from everything. Vegas, LA, shit, even Mexico!" Juice said and started laughing.

DING!

Maria: *"Babe I'm here."*

DING!

She dropped her pin.

Los: *"yup lmk when you leave."*

"That right there, my boy, was the second to last piece of the puzzle. Now ol' Eddy is finna lead us to everything! You said Phoenix wide open? We gon' have to set up shop!" Los said and took his shot.

"That's what the fuck I'm talking 'bout!" Juice told him.

HP walked into the living room. "My niggas, what's the move?" HP said and sparked the Backwood in his hand.

"We finna hit that bitch Mona's uncle," Los told him.

"Bro, Juice, this nigga is a demon foreal!" HP said, thinking about Mona getting hit hella times with that nail gun. "You going to Home Depot again?" HP and Los started cracking up.

"Home Depot?" Juice asked, confused.

"Blood, this sick-ass nigga shot the bitch at least 30 times with' a fucking nail gun!" HP told him.

"A nail gun? God daaamn, Blood," Juice said.

"Crush your enemies totally. Mentally, physically, emotionally," Los said to them, quoting *48 Laws of Power*. Then told Juice what happened.

***

Maria and Eddy got to the apartment in Happy Valley, at the top of the hill on Johnson Creek.

Maria looked around the bachelor pad and took a seat on the couch. Eddy obviously lived alone. A mismatched couch and La-Z-Boy were the only furniture. He had a TV on the wall and a cigarette-burned coffee table.

So much money, but poor taste.

He grabbed the remote and turned on the TV. He flipped through channels and left it on slow mariachi music.

He pulled out a big bag of powder and dumped some of it onto the coffee table and made lines for both of them.

The ride from the club in Gresham to the apartment in Happy Valley took about 20 minutes. The whole drive Eddy was drinking a bottle of Mezcal tequila from Mexico and singing Spanish love songs to Maria. By the time they got to the apartment, he was lit.

"You like to party, chica?" Eddy asked her as he sniffed a long line off the table. "Aahh. Very good!" He didn't wait for her to answer. He handed her the $100 bill he was using as a tooter.

She took the bill and said, "This is my first time." Lying her ass off!

"Well then! This a night for firsts! *Vamanos!*" Eddy told her.

Maria lowered her face to the coffee table, put the bill to her nose and sniffed the line. She felt her face go numb and the hairs on her body stood up. Her pussy instantly was soaked. She squeezed her legs together and handed the tooter back to him.

"Good shit, eh? I got the best *cocaina* in the West Coast!" Eddy boasted.

"What is it you do?" Maria asked him.

"I'm the boss of La Familia Cartel, *mija. El jefe!*" he said and beat his fist on his chest.

If her aunt hadn't filled her in about Eddy, she would've been impressed. But she knew the truth and thought he was a clown.

Eddy leaned down to sniff another line, he inhaled, sat back and handed her the bill. He got up and salsa danced his way to the kitchen. He grabbed another bottle of tequila from the cupboard. He grabbed two shot glasses and salsa danced his way back to the living room.

Maria definitely wasn't trying to get drunk and lose control of herself or the situation, so she grabbed his hand and led him to the bedroom.

She sat him down on the bed and started pulling his pants down, eager to get this over with. She pulled out his dick and had to stop herself from laughing at the size of it. She grabbed it and started sucking him slowly, and almost gagged from the taste. She thanked God he got hard right away. She stood up and slid her dress up, over her hips.

Eddy loved what he saw. He sat up and started sucking on her titties while he played with her wet box.

After a few moments she stopped him and went and layed down on the bed. She looked up at him while she pushed her fingers in and out of her pussy. The coke and alcohol had her pussy betraying her! She was horny and getting wetter!

He layed his sweaty head between her legs and ate her pussy like a pro! "Oh my God," Maria yelled as she came in his mouth.

Eddy flipped her on her stomach and entered her from behind. *This can't be the same dick I just had in my mouth*, she thought.

Just like the drugs and alcohol had her soaking wet, it made his lil' man into a bigger man. He started drilling her! Pounding away, stomach bouncing up and down on her ass cheeks, sweat dripping down onto her back from his face. Maria was gripping the sheets. She couldn't stop herself from throwing it back at him! Ten seconds later she heard his breathing change, then felt him nut in her! He pulled out, flopped onto the bed and was out cold!

Maria looked at him, then got up and went into the bathroom to clean herself. She was pissed that she didn't use protection! But at least she was on birth control.

She went back to the bedroom and poked him to see if he would wake, but he was out! She picked up his pants and took the knot of hundreds he was flexing earlier. She went to the living room and sniffed another long line before putting the powder back into the bag and putting it and the money into her purse. She grabbed her heels and tip-toed silently to the door.

Fuck!

She remembered his man had her car. She went to the parking lot and saw his security sitting in the Escalade. Parked next to it was her Audi. She walked to the driver-side window and he handed her the keys and smiled at her.

"The night doesn't have to end, Mami." He flashed his gold-outlined teeth to her and smirked.

She grabbed her keys from him and smiled back. "Sorry. I don't fuck the help," she told him.

As she walked behind the truck she fake-dropped her purse, so she could kneel down and put the GPS magnet under the bumper.

The vato in the truck seen this and laughed at her drunken clumsiness. “Pinche puta,” he said as she gathered her things.

She got in her car, started it, and backed out of the parking spot. She looked at him looking at her and she flipped him off. Her heart was still beating a mile a minute when she got to the 205 freeway.

She called Los as she drove. He forwarded her call. *Fucking asshole*, she thought and called him back. She was ready to blow him up if he sent her to voicemail one more time!

He picked up. “What’s good, baby? You good?” he asked her.

“Oh my God, babe! He’s fucking gross!” she told him.

Los laughed and said, “You took one for the team! I’m proud of you though! You handled your business like a real bitch.”

“Thanks, papi. Are you coming over?” she asked him, already knowing the answer would be no.

“Shit. I don’t know. I’ma let you know though. But aye! I gotta go. Text me when you get home.”

“Fine,” she said and hung up.

Maria had planned for this, and planned on getting him over there tonight by any means necessary. She opened up her purse and took a picture of the money and drugs she stole from Eddy. She sent the picture to Los in a text saying: *“still don’t know if you’re coming TN?”*

DING!

She smiled when she read his reply: *“See you later!”*

***

Los looked at the picture Maria sent him. *This bitch puts in work,* he thought to himself.

"Let's wrap this shit up. I'm finna pull up with Boog tomorrow though, and we gon' run the play by him," Los told them.

"It's good. Hit yo white boy though. Let's grab some new heats for this," Juice said.

HP agreed with him. "On God. Put in an order, brother."

"I got y'all niggas," Los said. "Juice, you finna stay here?"

"Yeah, I'm finna post up. My BM been tripping since before I left," Juice told him and shook his head. "After we do this shit, I'm finna get my own spot on the bitch! Have her come over just to kick her funky ass out! Leave the kids here though, bitch!" They all started laughing at that.

"Aight, it's good. I'ma get with y'all niggas tomorrow," Los said, then stood up. He shook both of them up with the B, then headed toward the door and stopped. He turned around and said, "You niggas almost had me for my fast charger!" Then went to the wall and unplugged it.

"Nigga, fuck that charger," HP said.

"Yeah, I know," Los said and left.

HP locked the door up behind him. "Run the 2K. $100 a game," he looked at Juice and said.

"$100 a game? Nigga, say less!" Juice said and grabbed the sticks.

***

"You did a good job tonight," Los said to Maria as he counted Eddy's money she took for him. "I'm proud of you. Shit like this bring us closer foreal."

Maria beamed at the compliment. She lived to please this nigga.

Maria got behind him and started rubbing his shoulders and kissing his neck. "I love you, papi," she told him in between kisses.

"Is that right?" Los asked her.

"That's right, my love," Maria answered. "Since day one."

"I love yo loyalty. But you gotta get your ass in the shower. You smell like a fat Mexican right now!" he told her playfully, then put his hand up to cover his nose.

"Babe, stop!" Maria said, then put her pout face on and swung a pillow at him.

Los ducked, then picked her up and slammed her onto the bed. His face was inches from hers. "See baby, I wanna be kissing all on you right now, be all on you right now, but you still got that fat fuck's scent all over you. Hold up. Did you let that muthafucka bareback you?" he asked her.

"Of course not!" she panicked and lied quickly.

He got up from the bed and grabbed his scale from his Prada backpack to weigh the coke she brought him. "Like I said though. Go hop in that water."

She didn't say anything. He turned around and seen her staring at him.

"Weirdo. What you waiting on?" he asked her.

She huffed and puffed her way to the bathroom and slammed the door. She connected her phone to the Bluetooth speaker and played *"Tink - Somebody."*

He laughed when he heard the song, 'cause he knew she was subbing him. *Soft ass,* he said to himself and laughed.

DING!

Kaleah: "Are you okay?"

Los: "Yeah baby. Be there soon."

Kaleah: "K. Love you."

Los: "Love u more!"

He put the phone down. *Kaleah? That was his real love! Fasho!*

He looked down at the scale: 53 grams.

Okay, baby brought me damn near 2 zips! He put his house key in the sack and pulled out a big ass scoop, put it to his nose and inhaled. *Fuck! This is some gas!*

He dipped the key in the bag, pulled out and inhaled again.

Maria got out the shower and seen him putting the scale, powder, and money into his Prada bag.

"Where are you going?" she asked.

"I'm finna go make this move. Did he get yo number, license plate, any of that?"

"I'm not sure. Why?"

"Kuz this shit finna get real." He went into his bag, took 3 bands out and gave it to her. "Take this and go visit yo grandma for a few weeks."

She went to say something, but he cut her off before she could get the words out. "Look, you think he's finna wake up and not notice 15k and 2 zips of raw missing? Don't be hardheaded, Maria. Take this money and dip." He shook his head. "See, this why I don't be concerned about you bitch. Kuz you don't listen. And if you don't care, I'm for damn sure not finna care."

He took the money out of her hands and threw it onto the bed and turned to leave. "And keep yo location on!"

She smiled at him. "Let me find out you love me." Then ran up and hugged him.

Don't get ahead of yourself, bitch, he thought.

She dropped to her knees and said, "I need a midnight snack before you leave," and blew him down.

After he shot his load down her throat, he went to take a piss. When he came out, she handed him the 3k back. "I hit for some money on VP tonight. Keep this, papi."

She handed him the money and sent him on his way to his main bitch.

Chapter 14

Los opened his eyes to an ear-piercing scream.

AAGGHHH!

The scream came again. He looked over and seen Kaleah wasn't there. He got up and ran towards the sound.

He got to the hallway and seen the walls of the Airbnb were covered with pictures of different murder scenes. In the pictures were people he murdered personally and people close to him that had been killed.

What the fuck, he thought as he looked from picture to picture, seeing Mona slumped in the chair, front of her body covered with nails and half of her face missing.

The next picture was his brother, Slim Ru, falling to the ground after getting hit by a lucky shot from a nerd-ass nigga. He got killed for being a real nigga in the right place at the wrong time.

He shed tears.

There was an unseen force guiding him to the living room. He was drawn to it. He rounded the corner and lost his breath at what was before him.

Juice was standing there bleeding from bullet wounds to the chest, shoulder, legs, and face. He was laughing. He said, *"See you soon, brother."* But it wasn't his voice. The words coming out sounded low, raspy, and scratchy. Like death.

The TV was playing on repeat a clip of his closest homie hitting heavy at a dice game. Then the next clip was him on the ground, paralyzed after back and leg shots. Looking his own blood in the eyes before he left him to bleed out.

That same force pushed Los' body to the left, and 17 dead people from the park shooting were staring at him accusingly with dead, vacant eyes.

He saw a set of twin toddlers jerking on the floor from .223 shells. Dead before they hit the ground, while their mother died trying to shield them with her body. His heart broke for his dead homies and the other young lives lost.

WOOOOSH!

A chair was slid underneath him, and he was violently sat down. The TV appeared in front of him and he was looking at a first-person view of him getting shot up, then of Kaleah getting shot in his car and crashing.

He started jerking in the chair, sweating, out of breath, struggling. Trying to get free and turn the TV off. Not wanting it to be real.

WOOOOSH!

The unseen force pushed against his chest and was shaking him 'til he was out of breath and blacked out...

***

"Babe!" Kaleah yelled as she shook Los, trying to wake him from the violent nightmare he was having. She woke up to him gripping the blanket, struggling to breathe. She shook him and beat against his chest 'til he woke.

"AAGGHHH!" he yelled and sat up in the bed, breathlessly. He looked around the room and remembered his dream. He grabbed the pump from under the bed frame and went to the hall and into the living room. He came back feeling relieved.

"Fuck, babe," he said as he sat down at the foot of the bed. He set the shotgun at his feet. "I fucking hate it here," he told her, referring to Portland.

"I know, baby. Me too. Let's leave," she told him. "We're already paying for a fucking Airbnb. Let's pay for our stuff to be moved to a storage and let's just go. We'll send for it later." She scooted to the end of the bed and laid her head down on his shoulder.

"You know what, Lee? I'm down. Give me a couple days to wrap things up and let's dip. A fresh start. Start looking at places," Los told her.

"Are you foreal?" Kaleah asked him.

He took her face in his hands and said, "I'm so foreal. Don't question it." Then kissed her lips.

She kissed him back, then said, "Where, babe?" excitedly.

"Arizona. Look for houses outside of Phoenix. Scottsdale, Casa Grande, Tempe. Areas like that," Los responded.

"Yes! Babe, can my caregiver come? She's paid for the next 2 months and I like having her around. That's my friend foreal," Kaleah said.

"Man, what's up with that girl? I'm surprised she's not here right now. She living here now? What do y'all be doing?" Los questioned.

"Well, for starters she's helping me get full range of motion in my arm again. We talk a lot about life and goals. She's very smart—went to law school, ya know? I've been thinking about going to college to do something in that field also," she answered.

"What does *something in that field* mean? You tryna be a lawyer or DA? Enforce the law and shit? I hope you don't be telling this bitch our business," he said to her with a frown.

"No. Never. I know how you live, babe, and would never go against the grain. Maybe like criminal justice. Be a voice for the voiceless," she said.

"I dig it. Listen, Lee, live yo dream, baby. I'm not mad at it. I'm here for the ride with you!" Los looked her in the eyes and said.

"Till the wheels fall off," she finished his sentence.

Now this was a woman he loved to death. His future was clear. He just had to get Eddy and Bird out of the way. It was too dangerous letting them live.

"I'm down for Kayla to stay the 2 months. No longer though. She gives me a weird feeling. Something off with that girl," Los said.

"Baby, everybody gives you a weird feeling! You're just paranoid," Kaleah told him.

"Yeah yeah. I'ma fly y'all out there today though. Get your stuff ready. Find an Airbnb in Casa Grande," he told her.

"K, babe!" Kaleah jumped up and kissed him.

***

With both of his bitches out the way, Los could focus on the task at hand. Which was: the 20k play from Dolce, and knocking Eddy and Bird off the chessboard, then taking everything in the warehouse.

That dream still had him shook, lowkey. So much death. His past and present were full of violence, it had him feeling like death was around the corner.

He never confronted his own mortality. He didn't have the time to second-guess his moves or decisions. The stakes were getting higher every day, and it was truly do or die.

Having Kaleah leave to AZ was perfect timing and took some weight off his shoulders. Kaleah was really his homie, lover, friend.

Maria just was what she was. Now, Los definitely appreciated how down she was and her head game went crazy! But at the end of the day, she was just another tool in his box.

He was grateful Kaleah didn't press him about the nightmares, even though she was concerned. He texted Juice: *U n HP take 1st shift on Eddy.*

Say less! Juice responded.

He kicked off his Gucci slides and slid into some Gamma 11s. He grabbed a blue Gatorade out the fridge and was out the door, into traffic.

***

"My guy," Kobe said as Los walked into the basement workshop. "You hit me last minute, but I think I've got you covered," he told him, referring to the gun order Los had called in an hour earlier. Ghost guns to be specific. Untraceable. His boy did everything on a 3D printer in his soundproof workshop he set up in his basement.

Kobe picked up an Army duffel bag and set it on the table and motioned for Los to come over and check out the contents.

Los looked into and picked through the items approvingly. The bag held a pair of 1911 .45s that had their firing pins and barrels swapped, and a switch on the back turned it into an automatic. Two baby AR-15 assault rifles with fiber optic scopes and beams on them, with nylon chest straps attached to carry them cross-body without holding them. There were extra clips, magazines, 2 lightweight Kevlar vests, and the suppressors he asked for.

"I'll take it all," Los said.

"5k. It's good," Kobe responded.

"Say less, my good man." Los counted out 5k from the money Maria had given him the night before and laid it on the table.

"These muthafuckas is nice," Los said, picking up the Baby A. He slapped a clip in and racked the lever back, putting one up top. He popped the shell out and put it back where it belonged, then back in the bag.

"Always good doing business with you, bro," Los said, then pulled another 7k out his crossbody bag. "Here go 7 bandz, bro. Make a to-go bag for me with the same shit in it. Juice gon' come grab it. The extra 2 bandz is for next time I pull up. I want a couple Glock 20s made. Desert Camouflage," Los told him.

"I got you," Kobe said.

"Bet. Juice gon' be here in 'bout an hour." Los shook his hand and left the basement, hopping in a Tahoe he rented earlier that day with a different ID and credit card.

***

Los texted Boogie: *"he was outside so come on."* While he waited, he looked at the info Dolce had provided on the two targets again. The GPS said they were an hour away, hiding in Woodburn, Oregon.

DING!

Boogie: "3 mins Brody."

After reading that, he sent a text to Juice: *"you pick up the poles yet?"*

Juice: "just got em. Otw to Mexico RN."

Los: "how long 'til u there?"

Juice: "just pulled up. Finna park where I can see who come n go."

Los: "Good shit. Keep yo eyes on him."

Los sent that last text, then set his phone down. He looked up and Boogie was coming out of the building with a backpack in his hands. He opened the passenger door, threw the bag in the backseat, and got in. He was anxious to get away from this area. Boogie lived across the street from the sheriff's office in downtown Vancouver.

"Man, yo sis in there tripping, Blood," Boogie said as he rolled down the window and sparked a port.

"You niggas always arguing with the bitch. Bet if you let her instead of sweat her for a few days, she gon' get some act right," Los kicked game to his homeboy. "Bitch gon' shit on the pot or get off it fucking with Loso!"

Los then opened up the center console and took out the burner phone. He pulled up the info and handed it to Boogie so he could familiarize himself with the situation.

"In a quarter mile, turn right onto I-5 and continue for 47 miles," Siri said over the speakers.

"Damn, these muthafuckas was major. Did you read this shit?" Boogie asked him.

"Yeah. Once these muthafuckas out the way and ol' boy comes home on appeal, this gon' be our way in the door of the big leagues," Los said as he scrolled through Apple Music looking for a song. He picked Yatta's *Messy Murder Scene* and turned the volume up.

"Lil nigga heavy metal messy murder scene. Looked in that boy's eyes when I murdered him. 10k and it all came from a burglary. Another sucka died and I love the nigga that murdered him."

This song always put Los in killer mode.

"You feel me though, bro? Caesar got caught in a load with' 20 birds, a Drako, and a million cash. These brothers put all the blame on him, so he got all day pretty much. Once they gone and he come home, he gon' put us on foreal. Just watch my boy. Real niggas do real things. Plus he up there with' Cream. I just sent bro a text telling him tap in."

"I feel it," Boogie said. "Nigga, if it was me driving? I woulda never stopped! Sound like a set up to me! How kuddy doing up there though?"

"On dead homies," Los agreed. "He good though. Just staying down for his crown. One thing about bro is, he gon' see it through."

"Gee-oh-Dee. I'ma send him a juug after the bitch pay us," Boogie said.

"Yup. I'ma let him know."

Twenty minutes later, they got off the freeway at the Woodburn exit and turned right at the light. They drove a few blocks into a residential community, continuing to the back of the homes. They drove by the brothers' house with the windows rolled up. They couldn't risk being seen and losing the element of surprise. Lucky for them, the house was the furthest point between two street lights, so it was the darkest on the block.

They continued driving and stopped, parking on the street next to a park. They waited for it to get dark outside. The sun set 30 minutes later, the moon was out, and the street lights came on. It was go time.

Los grabbed the duffle bag from the back seat and sat it in his lap. He handed Boogie a Baby A, then a 1911 just in case. Then he pulled out one of the Kevlar vests and unzipped the front two pouches, sliding in the steel plates. He did it again for the other one and handed it to Boogie, along with a titanium suppressor to screw on the barrel of the rifle to silence it.

"Ooweee! This muthafucka right here, boy!" Boogie said, referring to the Baby AR-15.

"Put your vest on, nigga," Los told him, then threw a pair of black surgical gloves to him. They came with their own Nike Pro ski masks. They strapped the Baby A's to their bodies and zipped their hoodies over them.

"You ready, brother?" Los looked Boogie in the eyes as he asked this, hoping he didn't see any hesitation in them.

He felt relief and pride when Boogie answered, "I came ready, brother. We go in together, we leave together."

"No question," Los replied, then pulled his skizzy down over his face.

Los double-checked that his phone was off. He double-checked Boogie's as well, then locked them in the glove box.

Earlier they had done another pass-by and seen the house to the right of the targets was empty. Los Google Earthed it and saw a fence separating the two yards.

They drove down the street with the headlights off, slowly, and pulled into the driveway of the empty house and parked in the garage. They left the garage door open a few inches from the ground so it wouldn't lock into place.

They left the garage and crept through the dark yard to the fence. It was six feet tall but stood on a cinder block base that made it closer to eight feet.

They waited a few minutes, listening and checking out the scene, memorizing the sounds of the environment.

They stepped into the base and swung the rifles to their backs, not wanting them to get caught on the fence when they went over. They grabbed the top and pulled themselves over, landing softly in the grass.

"Fuck!" Juice said to HP. "The text aint delivering!"

They were watching Eddy and a car full of security at the exit gate, waiting to go through.

"Fuck it. Let's go," Juice said as the truck drove by them. He started the Camaro and followed them from a safe distance.

Eddy pulled onto the freeway entrance heading north and sped up once he merged into traffic. He was switching lanes like he knew he was being followed.

Juice hit the gas on the Camaro, getting up to 110 mph before he was close enough to the truck again.

VROOM!

They flew by a state trooper.

"Fuck!" Juice yelled, looking at the trooper pulling into traffic with his lights on from his rearview. The sounds of the siren came next.

"Nigga, aint no way we pulling over! All that shit in the back! And we in a Maro! Fuck no!" HP said.

"Fuck, bro," Juice yelled again and slammed his hand on the wheel. "Look, bro. I got my L's, my insurance good. I'ma pull over. Just stay calm."

HP looked at him like, nigga, are you crazy?

Juice eased off the gas and went to pull over.

HP grabbed a Baby A and racked the lever before sitting it between his body and the door. No way was he letting them take him back to jail!

The state trooper got out of his patrol vehicle and slowly walked to the Camaro with his palm resting on the butt of his service weapon.

He tapped on the window, telling Juice to roll it down. "Know how fast you were going back there, boy?" the trooper asked him. He saw the tattoos covering the neck and faces of both men in the car and judged them instantly. "Sir, actually, you and your passenger step out of the vehicle."

"For what? Speeding?" Juice asked him, sick.

The trooper brought his radio to his mouth, calling for backup, giving the location and description of the car and its occupants.

"Sit back, bro," HP whispered.

Juice looked at him and knew he was right. With the guns, suppressors, and vests, they'd get at least 20 years in the feds. That wasn't an option. Juice knew the trooper had to die, and his actions caused it.

"Sir, this is my last time asking you. Now GET THE FUCK OUT OF THE CAR!" the trooper yelled and made the mistake of moving his hand to draw down.

Juice threw his seat back, and HP fired into the trooper's belly, chest, and neck.

BRAAAAT! BRAAAAT! BRAAAAT! BRAAAAT!

The trooper was in shock, trying to put his intestines back into his stomach.

BRAAAAT! BRAAAAT! BRAAAAT!

HP fired again, killing him.

"Nigga, go!" HP yelled.

Juice threw the Maro into drive and took off, merging back into nighttime traffic, searching for an exit to get off at. They had to get rid of the Maro ASAP!

"I told you not to fucking pull over, bro! What's the point of having a Maro if you not finna go fast when it counts?" HP yelled. "We gotta go, bro. ASAP. Take the exit here and make a left on 97th and Foster. We gon' park this and take my babymoms' shit!"

Juice nodded his head, in shock, knowing this was all his fault.

"Call bro and tell him change of plans! He's finna be hot! This shit with Eddy is personal with him 'cause they shot his bitch!" Juice told HP.

HP dialed the number and it went straight to voicemail. Same with Boogie's phone.

They got there and Juice parked. He stayed in the car while HP ran inside and got the keys to his babymoms' Nissan and went into the basement and got a screwdriver and a tarp to cover the Camaro.

He got into the Nissan and pulled out of the driveway so Juice could pull in and park. He grabbed the screwdriver and took off both license plates, then covered the car from bumper to bumper with the tarp.

He grabbed the bag with the guns and shit and threw it in the backseat of the Nissan—close in case they needed it.

HP put the 2020 tinted gray Nissan Altima into drive and they drove out of the neighborhood.

"We gotta get the fuck outta here," HP said as a helicopter flew over them searching for the Camaro. The manhunt had already begun.

They drove through the city, avoiding the 205 freeway, where he just killed the trooper. He got to I-5 and headed south.

"Where to, brother?" HP asked Juice.

"To Phoenix, my boy..."

Chapter 15

Los looked at Boogie and nodded his head for Boogie to follow him. They had their hoodies unzipped and were carrying the Baby A's, ready to shoot anything that moved.

They reached the deck, and from the floor plan Los had memorized, he knew the entertainment room was right behind the glass in front of them. Up the hall from there was the stairs to reach the bedrooms.

He placed his ear to the windows and heard sounds from the TV and somebody laughing. He motioned for Boogie to come forward and whispered, "There's somebody watching TV right behind these curtains. I'm gonna try the door softly. If it's unlocked, we slide it open and go in there. You cover one side of the room, I'll do the other. Shoot anything moving." He looked him in the eyes while he spoke and again saw no fear or hesitation.

He tried the door; it was unlocked. He slid the glass back slowly and without a sound, spread the curtains and got a glimpse inside.

The TV was on, and there were 3 men in the room, so focused on the bad Spanish bitch on TV that they were unaware of death a few feet away.

Los closed the curtains and whispered to Boogie, "3 people in there. Assume they're strapped. We lay them down and clear every room."

Boogie nodded his head in understanding.

Los counted to 3 and opened the door.

Manuel Ortega decided to get up and get another Modelo from the fridge. He was walking by just as the curtain opened and got the surprise of his life.

SMACK!

Los hit him with the stick of the rifle, then grabbed him in a headlock. "Caesar says hello!" Los yelled just as Boogie followed him into the house and opened fire into the room.

BRAAAAT! BRAAAAT! BRAATATAT! BRAATATAT!

The brother of Manuel, Juan, was hit in the neck. He stood up and put his hand to his neck in shock as blood started spraying from the wound and he died.

Johnny jumped up and grabbed the old Russian AK leaning against the couch and returned fire, "*Pinche putos!*"

BRAAAAT! BRAAAAT! BRAAAAT!

Boogie ducked behind the wall into the hallway. Johnny was still firing. Los threw Manuel into the line of fire and started shooting.

BRAATATAT! BRAATATAT! BRAATATAT! BRAATATAT!

Manuel was hit from both front and back, spinning as the bullets tore into him.

"*Primo!*" Johnny screamed as he watched Manuel die.

He aimed at Los and squeezed the trigger. Nothing happened. A bullet was jammed. He smacked the lever trying to free it. Johnny panicked and rushed Los.

Los smiled. Boogie popped out from behind the wall and fired the same time Los did. They ate him up.

"You good?" Los looked at Boogie and said.

He nodded his head yeah.

"Good. Let's check out the rooms."

Boogie led the way upstairs. They got to the landing and went into the first bedroom. They flipped the mattress, went through the closet and found nothing.

Same with the next room.

They got to the third room and it looked like it was used for storage. Boxes everywhere. Los took the top off a green plastic storage container and his eyes got big at what he saw: stacks of gold bars, at least 12 of them.

"Boog! Hand me the bag! We hit!" Los yelled to him.

"On my Mama!" Boogie handed him the bag. "What else they got?"

They opened up more storage bins but found nothing.

"Let's go!" Los grabbed him.

They ran downstairs and stopped when they got to the dead bodies. Los took a photo of each victim as proof for Dolce.

They ran into the backyard and, filled with adrenaline, both of them cleared the fence with a hand on top of it to stabilize them.

They ran into the garage and Los opened the back door and slid the bag of gold underneath the seat.

Boogie slid the garage door up. Los pulled out, he hopped in, and they pulled off inconspicuously.

Los drove the speed limit through the neighborhood, amazed no cops were speeding by or no sirens in the distance. He got to the freeway and pushed the Tahoe to 90 on the way back to the town. "Damn! Get the phones and call Juice! I forgot all about them niggas!" Los told Boogie.

Boogie turned both phones on. "Damn. Hella missed texts and calls on both of 'em," Boogie said. He called Juice back. He answered on the first ring. Boogie was silent while Juice was telling him what happened. "Y'all did what?" Boogie exclaimed, hoping his ears heard wrong.

"Bro, put that shit on speaker," Los told him.

"Say that shit again, bro," Boogie said to Juice.

"Nigga, we knocked down a state trooper. There was no other way. He was calling backup and we got the poles and shit. It was the right move," Juice said, having HP's back.

"I feel you, Blood. But what the fuck! They got yo license plate, bro. It's finna be hot as fuck. Y'all niggas get low ASAP. Where y'all at?" Los asked him.

"We on the road. We switched loads. We on I-5 south, Blood," Juice told him.

"Hit me when you get where y'all going. Be smooth, bro! And get rid of that phone! HP too!" They hung up.

Los shook his head. "Them niggas are hot."

"Looks like it's me and you for the Eddy move," Boogie said.

Los checked the location of Eddy's truck. It was parked by the St. Johns Bridge in North Portland. "What the fuck they doing there?" Los said and handed Boogie the phone with the GPS still pulled up.

"Let's find out," Boogie said back.

"Say less," Los responded, ready to get Eddy out of the way.

It didn't matter if it was only him and Boogie. Quality over quantity. Them 2 niggas was ready to kill whoever.

Chapter 16

"I understand we have a common goal between us," Marky said to the man on the other end of the video call.

"And what is that?" the man asked.

"Removing Los and his team from this side of life," Marky answered.

"Ahh. The enemy of my enemy is my friend. I see the logic of your thinking. And also where you're going with this conversation. So, tell me why I need you to accomplish this task, and besides that, what do you bring to the table?" Bird asked.

"I kill him, I get his old seat. I can succeed where your men have failed. Plus, I know that Los played a major part in making your Portland market profitable. With all this shit he has going on, he can't possibly be hitting all his normal licks. Supply and demand. Those customers are finna be looking for someone to take his place as their supplier. I was raised in the game. I can be that," Marky told him confidently.

Bird thought about this for a moment, then said, "You know the penalty of failure? If he survives and doesn't kill you, I will. Group extermination. Do you understand this?"

"I do," Marky responded, all in. He just committed his brothers to either balling or falling.

"And you're confident and willing to risk the life of not only you, but the lives of your brothers?" Bird asked.

"The way I see it, we already risking our lives just living the way we do. Now it's time for that risk to be rewarded," Marky answered.

"Indeed. Very well. I'll send the location for you to pick up your first pack. Flip it, re-up. You have 2 weeks to get rid of our mutual problem, or I will get rid of you," Bird said and hung up.

He hoped that since Los used to be a Mobb member, Marky would know how he moved and be able to kill him. Los was causing Bird too many problems, and the financial ones were the least of them.

***

"Bitch, wait a minute," Liv said to Kaleah. "You're leaving to Arizona? Today? To look for a house?"

"Yess! It's all last minute. But since I got shot, I've been cooped up in the house and it's not even my house! We've decided that a fresh start would be best," Kaleah told her.

"I heard that. Well shit, let me buy my ticket, 'cause aint no way my lil sis is going without me!" Liv said.

"Sister, I love you! Book your flight on Southwest. We board at 9 p.m."

"I got you, sister! I love you!" Liv yelled.

They hung up, and Kaleah continued packing her things, excited for new beginnings. She sent a text to Kayla: *girl we leave n 2 hrs. wya?*

She put the phone down and thought about her man. She looked at the screensaver on her phone, a selfie she took of them at the beach. Never in her life had she felt a love like this. She knew Los was out handling business, so she didn't interrupt him. She was secure in her spot.

DING!

Kayla: sorry! Running late! I'll meet you there before we board!

Kaleah read the text from Kayla and shook her head, annoyed. She responded: *K,* and put her phone down.

DING!

She picked up her phone and looked at the text: *sis! just booked it! meet you before we board!*

Damn, that was fast, she thought. *K sister,* she replied to Liv.

20 minutes later, she was done packing. She checked the time: 7:35 p.m. She booked an Uber, and 10 minutes later she was on her way to the airport.

***

Eddy sat in the living room of the studio apartment while Malone and Lopez talked on the patio with the door closed. He was anxious to get this over with, for his brother to be locked up—better yet, dead—so he could be Jefe.

***

"Are you sure you'll be good all the way in Arizona?" Malone asked Lopez as they stood on the patio and discussed her departure.

"Yes. I'm positive. They don't suspect me to be anything more than a friend and a physical therapist. I'll check in when I can for an actual conversation with you. Other than that, I'll continue to leave messages on the drop number," she reassured him.

"Okay then, I'll clear it. Stay in touch and be careful. If I don't hear from you 2 weeks in a row, I'll contact my boy at the Phoenix field office and have him assess the situation on foot," Malone said.

"No! Don't tell Phoenix anything. Deep cover is deep cover. Start worrying after a month. But please let me work, Malone," Lopez pleaded with her superior.

Malone raised his hands in mock surrender. “Understood. Now let’s wire this piece of shit up and both of you can be on your way!”

They stepped into the apartment, and Malone spoke first. “Ready, amigo?”

He walked to a suitcase, opened it, and pulled out a tiny microphone with a wire connecting it to a transmitter. He grabbed a roll of double-sided tape and threw it to Lopez, who unrolled half a foot and sat the tape down.

Eddy felt like the rat he was. Then thought about his future as the Jefe and pushed all uncertainty aside.

“Take your shirt off,” Lopez told Eddy. Lopez handed Malone the tape and placed it on the device. He then placed the device on Eddy’s chest, close to his heart.

“So be within 5 feet of whoever you’re speaking to. Remember, for us to get convictions, we need clarity. Clarity means clear, amigo,” Malone told Eddy, then grabbed a chunk of chest hair and pulled.

Eddy grunted in pain. Malone laughed and let go.

“So, are we clear?” he asked him.

“Crystal clear,” Eddy replied. He grabbed his shirt and put it back on. “Anything else you dirty motherfuckers need? How about I wear this to my mother’s house next?”

“No. We’re good... for now,” Malone said.

Eddy left.

Lopez grabbed her jacket and walked toward the door. “I’ll be in touch. You be safe tonight, Malone.”

And she left the apartment, leaving him alone with his ambitions.

***

Los and Boogie pulled up to where the GPS said Eddy was and seen him coming out of the apartment alone.

“Should we snatch him up here?” Boogie asked.

"Nah. Let's follow this fat fuck to the payday. Fuck that apartment," Los told him, then closed his eyes for 10 seconds.

The adrenaline rush from earlier had worn off and he felt exhausted. If he would've kept them open, he would've seen Agent Lopez—known to him as Kayla—leave the same apartment 20 seconds after Eddy.

Boogie looked at Los and seen the bags underneath his eyes and felt pain for his bro. He looked like a man who had made many desperate decisions lately and lived through all of them.

"You good, brother?" he asked him.

Los opened his eyes. "Yeah bro. Let's get this shit over with."

He put the car in drive and headed toward the warehouse they drove by earlier.

Los seen Eddy's brake lights ahead and sped up to intercept him. He spoke, "Same plan. Just us. Let's be on point."

"We go in together. We make it out together," Boogie told him.

They shook hands. All in.

Eddy parked next to the building. As soon as he stepped out of the vehicle, Los pulled up and Boogie bounced out before the Tahoe stopped.

"Don't say a muthafucking thing," he growled and pointed the rifle at him.

Los was out and around the truck seconds later. He lifted his ski mask and showed Eddy his face. "Remember me?" he spat at him, then punched him in the face.

Eddy fell against the Escalade and put his hands up. "P-P-Please don't kill me," he stuttered.

"Into the warehouse, bitch." Los grabbed him and pushed him toward the door. When they reached it, he stopped him.

"How many people inside? Lie and you die!"

"J-Just 4," Eddy stuttered again, terrified.

Los motioned for Eddy to open the door. He did, and they pushed him in front of them into the building.

They entered and seen 4 men seated around a table with the money counter doing its job for them. Bags of money sat on the floor beside them, next to stacks of cocaine bricked up and hundreds of thousands of pills. The men at the table were relaxed, confident nobody would try them.

Silent in their entrance, Los and Boogie knocked down 2 of the 4 men at the table before they knew what was going on. The remaining 2 jumped up and reached for their weapons.

"Reach and your boss dies. Then you're next," Los said menacingly.

They hesitated, and Boogie shot one in the arm.

"AAGGHH!" he screamed.

"You reach, I teach," Boogie said matter-of-factly.

Los spoke to them. "My problem aint with you. It's with your boss and his brother. So be koo and you can make it home to your loved ones."

They relaxed at the mention of making it home.

Los pushed Eddy towards them. He stumbled and fell forward. He tried to get up but Los kicked him in the ass. "Stay down!" He did.

Los pulled 2 sets of zip ties from his pocket and threw them at Boogie. "Restrain them, bro." Los got up on them with the rifle to let them know any sudden movement was a death sentence.

Boogie grabbed the one he shot and pulled his arms behind him. He screamed out in pain. "AAGGHH!"

Los clubbed him in the head with the rifle, knocking him out.

"Much easier," Boogie said as he put the zip ties on him.

They looked at the other guy. He obviously wanted no trouble. He put his hands behind him willingly and was restrained.

"How much money is here?" Los asked him.

"200 thousand," he responded.

While this was going on, Eddy sat there, wondering if the wire was working, because why weren't the feds there to save his ass?

Los looked at him as Boogie put the drugs in the bags. He walked toward him. "Bet you regret the day you met me huh?" Los said and laughed. "If it makes you feel any better, I'm gonna murder your brother next."

He looked at Boogie. "We good to go, brother?"

Boogie gave him a thumbs up.

"Looks like your time on earth has come to an end, my friend," Los told Eddy and took aim.

"Wait! Wait! You can't kill me! I'm wearing a wire, Los!" Eddy yelled, saying Los' name purposely, hoping the wire caught it.

Los snatched Eddy's shirt and ripped it off him, exposing the device. "You snitch bitch!" he spat at him, then fired the Baby A into his face anyway.

THRAAATAATATAAT! THRAAATAATATAAT!

Eddy fell backwards, half his face gone, his body jerking.

Los looked at the 2 men tied up. "I'm a man of my word."

Him and Boogie both grabbed 2 bags—one filled with money, the other with drugs. They left them there zip tied.

As they were leaving, 3 men walked in with their own duffel bags to cop work. Los and Boogie recognized them instantly. Marky and 2 of his flunkies.

The 3 men looked at the 2 men in ski masks and at the dead bodies they were leaving behind. They reached for their weapons and both groups started firing at each other.

WOP! WOP! WOP! WOP! WOP!

THRAAT! THRAAATAATAT! THRAAT!

SMACK!

Los went down, hit hard in the chest. Boogie seen this and went crazy! He returned fire, hitting 2 of them. They dropped.

Marky retreated behind a row of wooden shipping containers, taking cover.

"Aw! Fuck!" Los yelled.

Taking the shot in the vest hurt like hell, but at least he wasn't dead. He crawled toward his gun just as Boogie ran out of shots.

Click. Click.

Boogie tried to fire, not realizing his clip was empty. Marky heard this and smiled. He came from behind the row of boxes and was met with gunfire.

THRAAATAATATAAT! THRAAATAATATAAT!

He was confused! He saw Los take the shot in his chest and go down.

But Los only had a bruised rib from the gunshot, but his aim was still off. He barely missed Marky.

Marky decided to live another day and dived out the window in front of him. He hit the ground and instantly scrambled for cover in the bushes next to the building.

Boogie ran over and helped Los get steady on his feet. They grabbed the bags and ran for the door.

They got to the car and heard the first siren. A few seconds later, they saw the red and blue lights.

Chapter 17

Los threw the bags in the backseat and got behind the wheel, ignoring the pain. He started the truck and Boogie got in. The truck was in reverse before he closed the door.

"Let's get the fuck outta here, nigga! Go! Go!" Boogie yelled.

Los took a right on Syracuse and drove up the hill. Banged a left on Ivanhoe and sped through the residential area. "Nigga, grab the chop!" Los yelled at Boogie, then hit the button for the sun roof. It slid back and Boogie had half his body out the truck seconds later. "Hold tight!" Los yelled as he took a hard right and sped past the 7/11, driving through the red light on Lombard.

Boogie started firing at the cops chasing them.

THRAATATAAT! THRAAATAAT! THRAAATATAAT!

The shells tore into the lead car's engine, causing it to stop abruptly. The cop car directly behind it hit the back of the stopped front car going 90 mph, caving in the lead car's trunk, forcing the second car on top of it, crushing the roof, killing the officers inside.

The remaining cars continued to follow them.

They made it past George Park and City Food Market. Going 110 mph, they hit the speed bumps and were in the air! Boogie almost dropped the rifle. He yelled down to Los, "Nigga! Where we going? Get us outta here!"

Los focused on driving and didn't respond.

Boogie fired into the windshield of the car that was gaining on them and hit the driver in the neck. His hand twitched on the wheel, turning it slightly, causing it to flip twice, landing on the sidewalk in front of the Taqueria on Fessenden.

Boogie dropped back down into the car and put a new clip into the Baby AR. “I love you, bro,” he told Los.

“I love you too, nigga. Now get yo ass back up there!”

Boogie climbed back out the sun roof and looked up at the helicopter that had joined the pursuit and started firing at it, trying to bring the ghetto bird down.

Los’ phone rang through the car speakers, it had connected to the Bluetooth when he got in. He looked down and seen who it was: Kaleah. Knowing he might not make it, he answered.

“Baby, we’re getting on the plane,” she told him.

“I love you, Lee. I’ll see you in a few days.”

THRAATATAAT! THRAAATAAT! THRAAATATAAT!

“Babe, are those gunshots in the background?” she asked him.

“Look, Lee, I gotta go! Hit me when you land! Just listen to me please!” Los said.

“Okay babe. I love you, okay? Make it home to me, okay?” she told him with emotion in her voice.

He hung up and focused back on the road.

PING! PING! PING!

Shots ricocheted off the Tahoe. The helicopter had a shooter that was firing back!

THRAATATAAT! THRAAATAAT! THRAAATATAAT!

Boogie fired into the cockpit of the helicopter relentlessly, causing it to momentarily stop pursuing them, pulling away.

Los took a hard left at 6 Point Bar. As he turned, the truck was on 2 wheels. It slammed hard back on the pavement, the force causing Boogie to drop the Baby A.

“Fuck!” he yelled, then climbed back down into the car, reaching for the bag of guns in the backseat.

“We almost there, brother. Just get ’em back off us one mo’ time,” Los told him.

Boogie popped back out and aimed the beam into the grill of the car and fired, hitting the engine. He kept his finger on the trigger 'til he saw smoke coming outta the grill.

Los took another left and sped through a gravel alley, kicking up dust. He braked hard.

"Get out and slide the garage up!"

Boogie bounced out and did it immediately, and Los pulled into the cover of the garage. Boogie slid the door down. They made it.

Los turned the car off and rested his head on the steering wheel.

Boogie sat on the ground with his back to the garage door, sweating, breathing hard.

The whirring of the helicopter was back, and there were sirens everywhere. But they were good.

"Who's shit is this, bro?" Boogie asked him.

"This my brother shit. He outta town right now though, we good," Los told him then got outta the truck and walked over to Boogie, sitting down next to him.

"We did that shit, brother. And we made it out alive!" Los told him and stuck his hand out.

We all in!"

Boogie shook it. "Ball or muthafucking fall, my nigga."

***

Malone heard the shots from the studio apartment a few blocks away, and was out the door and on the way to the warehouse moments later. No way a gunfight this close on this night was a coincidence.

He hadn't put the headphones on and start listening to the wire yet because he didn't expect anything to happen this early. This case could make or break his career and he couldn't afford to lose his star snitch!

As he was running to the warehouse, he heard the sirens and seen the first responding cars blow by him seconds later.

He saw the police chase begin from 50 yards away and knew in his gut that he was going to have to explain to his boss what went wrong. He was prepared for the worst but hoping for the best.

He got to the open door of the warehouse and seen the bodies on the floor. His heart sank when he saw Eddy on the floor dead, shirtless.

"Fucking A!" he screamed and heard the echo in the empty building.

He thought quickly and pulled the device off Eddy's chest and pocketed it before the Portland Police locked the scene down and started asking unnecessary questions.

He called Lopez and got her voicemail. He tried again and got the same result. *Must be on the plane*, he thought.

He went through Eddy's pockets and confiscated his phone. He thought about staying at the scene, but thought better of it and left the way he came—slipping into the darkness. *Let the local boy clean up this mess*, he thought.

Chapter 18

Los and Boogie were in the living room of the Townhouse with the money, drugs, and gold bars displayed in front of them on the coffee table.

"Now tell me one time you came up like this fucking with the Mobb niggas? Never mind! Don't answer that! Just come home, brother! We definitely got a jersey with yo name on it!" Los said as he paced the room excitedly.

Boogie looked at Los, then at the small fortune in front of him. "I'm with you, my boy."

"Shit, you better be! We just killed like 10 niggas! Shot it out with the boys! Nigga, you tried to shoot down a helicopter! Gangsta shit foreal! It's unfortunate that bitch nigga Marky got away but at least they down 2 more suckas! Check it out though, bro. You probably already know this, but I'm a real nigga so I gotta let you know what you signing up for. We outgunned, we outmanned, and this shit we took from them aint shit to these cartel niggas! On the dead homies! But we got a team of wolves! And we hungry! We gon' have to be strategic about every move kuz of them reasons, brother. But we gon' hit 'em where it hurts every time, my boy. And the one thing they won't do is outthink us!" Los preached.

As Boogie sat and listened to his friend, he knew he made the right decision and was going to ride or die for this Mafia shit.

"So what's next?" he inquired as Los continued pacing, smoking a Newport.

"Arizona, my boy. Juice and HP on they way. My bitch and her sis on a flight right now with her homegirl. We gon' leave in a few days. You with it?" Los asked him.

"I'm with it," Boogie said sincerely.

Los looked at Boogie and smiled. "My muthafucking nigga! Oh shit! Let me hit the bitch for the 20k. Have her pull up."

Los ran to the car and grabbed the burner phone. He texted Dolce the pictures of Manuel, Juan, and the dead relative. He dropped his pin.

She texted back seconds later and said she was on the way.

Los walked back into the living room and sat across the table from Boogie.

"Brother, when this bitch get here with the dub, be kool. She bad. Like the bitch Brittanya's twin. But badder! I'm probably finna taste that!" Los said and laughed.

"Nigga, don't shoot her when she choose The Boog!"

"Bitch ass nigga! Please!" Los said and threw a pillow from the couch at him.

Boogie ducked. "Nah foreal though, P. Fuck that bitch. All this shit in front of us. Niggas is on!"

"Yeah, it's definitely a start. Back to what I was just saying though. See, to us, this is a fortune. But to them, this is but a drop in the bucket. They not even gon' miss this, Blood. But you know what they will miss? Something unreplaceable. Family! When they shot my bitch, they crossed a line and it aint no going back! Nothing is off limits, my nigga. This shit is personal, Boog!" Los yelled the last part, getting angry. "We aint took no L's yet, and Lord willing, we don't. But the hard truth is not everybody gon' make it. We took a piece off the board tonight. We gon' knock another off before we leave to AZ." Los finished, then stood up and started putting shit back in the bags. "Help me put this shit up before the bitch get here with' the bag. She don't need to know anything more than what she supposed to."

After moving the bags back to the Tahoe, Los went to the kitchen to find something to eat, and Boogie went back to the living room. He sat on the couch and turned the TV on to Channel 12 news to see what the word was.

"*Breaking news out of Portland tonight...*"

His jaw dropped when he saw the pictures of Juice and HP leave the screen to show theirs. "Bro, I think you better see this shit!" he yelled out to Los.

Nayarit, Mexico

Juan sat in front of his computer, hacking into random crypto accounts and transferring the Bitcoin into accounts he ran for La Familia.

He put the fire to his meth pipe, spun it, and inhaled—it was gonna be a long night. Before he dropped out of MIT to come work for La Familia, he found that meth helped him focus better than Adderall. He also loved the high.

BEEP! BEEP!

His custom supercomputer had a notification. When he read it, his eyes got big and he grinned, knowing this was important to El Jefe.

He picked up his phone and dialed a number.

After a few rings, Bird picked up. "Que Paso?"

"Jefe, I got something you're going to love hearing."

"Then get on with it."

"Kaleah Bay used her personal debit card to book a flight from PDX to Sky Harbor in Phoenix. Her plane lands at 11:30 tonight."

Bird was quiet for a moment while he thought about this. "You've done good, mijo. Figure out where she's staying and also who shes traveling with. Get back to me ASAP."

As Bird was giving him instructions, another call came in on his phone. He answered.

"Jefe! Eddy is dead! They robbed us! Came in with masks and AK's! Tied me and Pablo up, killed Ricky and Tomas! We ran out the back before the federales showed up. Pero,

Jefe, Eddy was wearing a wire... your brother was an informat!" Eddy's head of security told Bird.

Before Malone showed up, he had managed to shake Pablo awake. They helped each other stand up, then ran out the back of the warehouse.

When they got a few blocks away, they used a Bic lighter to burn through each other's zip ties, setting themselves free.

"A fucking wire?" Bird screamed into the phone and threw his glass of liquor at the wall, shattering it. Scaring the whore he had over keeping him company. He left the room for privacy and said, "Tell me everything."

"Eddy left. He said he had something personal to handle. He came back 30 minutes later as a hostage. They killed Ricky and Tomas, shot Pablo when he tried for his gun. They zip tied us and were leaving when 3 Blacks came in to re-up and they shot it out. Killing them also. Then they left!" he finished, hoping these weren't his last days.

Working for the Cartel was a tricky business. The turnover rate due to death was high.

"Any idea who these men were?"

"No, Jefe! They were masked up! But I seen the wire with my own eyes. Before they killed him, he screamed that he was wearing a wire so please don't kill him! They ripped his shirt off and there it was."

"Gracias, Hermano. Tell nobody what you witnessed tonight. Get to a safe house and lay low. I'll call you with instructions manana." Bird hung up. *A fucking wire,* he thought. Then he wondered, *how long was Eddy snitching?*

Whoever killed him did Bird a favor. But their mother would be heartbroken, so they would have to die. Slow deaths, to be certain.

He would go to the family ranch and let her know in person. Tomorrow though. Tonight he had plans with his favorite whore.

Chapter 19

CLINK! CLINK!

The shovel sounded as it finally hit something besides the Earth. For the last 2 hours the 2 men had been shoveling up piles of dirt trying to reach this casket.

"Bro, come down here!" the one digging yelled up to the one keeping watch.

He dropped down into the hole and started to clear the dirt off the casket. They opened up the top half and a cloud of rotting flesh hit them in the face.

"Fuck, that's foul," he said, coughing and gagging at the smell. "Bro is a sick ass nigga for this!"

The other man laughed and agreed with him.

They stood on the bottom half of the casket, looking down at the lifeless corpse.

"This mine!" one of them exclaimed, snatching the 24 karat gold praying hands pendant and chain from her neck and pocketing it.

"Hand me the electric saw, P," he said to him. Once he had it in his hands, he turned it on and started cutting the head off the body.

Once they had it off, they wrapped it in a linen towel and stuffed it into a bag they brought. They climbed out of the hole and started refilling it with dirt.

***

“Today we’re here to give thanks for the many glorious things Eduardo did in his time on Earth and to celebrate the life that was cut short.”

Eddy’s mom was in the front row weeping silent tears, but she kept her composure. As the matriarch of the family, she had to show strength.

This was a small family church service. Invite only. Considering what had happened at Mona’s candlelight, this seemed the safest.

With only family attending, the security was minimal. Just 2 men posted inside the front door to the church. Bird didn’t come. The safest place for him was Mexico.

BOOM!

The doors to the church flew open! The 2 men stationed at the door were caught off guard. They reached for their weapons and were cut down before they cleared their holsters.

BRAAAAT! BRAAAAT! BRAAAAT! BRAAAAT!

Eddy’s mom jumped up as her security was gunned down and fearlessly addressed the 2 masked men.

“In a church! Have you cowards no morals!” she screamed angrily.

They walked down the aisle towards her, menacingly, and stopped 20 feet away.

Paris reached into the bag, pulled out Mona’s head and rolled it like a bowling ball to Eddy’s mom’s feet. It stopped face up. She looked down at her granddaughter’s face and fainted at the gruesome sight. She barely recognized her. There was valid reasons for her closed casket service.

Peezy fired into the air.

BRAAAAT! BRAAAAT! BRAAAAT!

Kapone ran up to the casket and fired into Eddy’s lifeless body, then kicking his casket off the table, making the body fall out face first. This shocked the crowd.

After doing this, they ran back out of the church, to a waiting car, ready to take them to the airport.

***

Caesar and Dolce sat in the visiting room, looking like 2 love birds that hadn't seen each other in a long time.

"So Johnny is dead tambien?" he asked her.

"Yes baby. He was with Manuel and Juan at the house when the party planners arrived. Did you know something I didn't, papi?"

Caesar looked at her, trusting her completely. "My lawyer told me there was a 3rd person feeding the feds information. But since he wasn't arrested, his name was never on paper. Information only somebody at the top would know. I had a feeling my brother was snaking me. I guess it was true. On a brighter note, I go up for my appeal next month."

"Then you're home!" Dolce said excitedly.

"Si, mi amor. Now that I'm Jefe, I'll be seeing about bringing Los into our organization. He gets the job done."

Dolce was also impressed with Los. They owed him big time. $20k was a small price to pay for Caesar's freedom.

"Have you heard from him since you helped get them outta Oregon?"

"No baby. I can contact him anytime. I gave him a new burner phone when I left him," she told Caesar.

"Let him know I send my love, respect, and gratitude. And that his family is coming home next. My word."

"Visit's over!" the hating ass bitch at the desk said.

They stood up, embraced, and parted ways.

Caesar got back to the unit and went to Cream's cell to chop it up.

"My dawg! What that lawyer talking about?" Cream said to Caesar.

"Good news. Their case was already weak. Now with the witnesses gone, I should be going home," Caesar told him.

"Good shit, good shit. Appreciate yo wife for getting my people out that jam foreal!" Cream said.

“Real ones do real things. We’re happy to help, brother. When I come home, you’ll be behind me shortly. You ready for the next level?” Caesar asked him.

“Am I?” Cream said. “Shit, I been ready! I let people judge me off my actions though, not my words.”

“And that is why you have my eternal love and respect. You and your family are going to be welcomed in to the Organization the right way. Your cousin's blood, sweat, and tears made this possible. Our future is bright together.”

“Indeed it is...”

Chapter 20

"Now that everybody is here, I want to make an announcement," Los said. They were seated in the basement of the mansion Airbnb in Casa Grande, Arizona.

The gang was lounging, fresh from a BBQ upstairs. The women were cleaning up while the men went downstairs to discuss business.

"All of us in this room has put in work in a major way these last couple weeks. The blood, sweat, and tears weren't for nothing. We're being welcomed into an Organization that will make us all richer than our wildest dreams, but we're still Mafia. That's the home team forever.

Them La Familia niggas thought we were some suckas, but they found out the hard way—the bloody way—that we're definitely not. I appreciate every single one of you. Everybody in this room is my brother. As a token of my appreciation, I gift y'all these."

Los then handed each of them a bag with 50k and two 50-ounce gold bars. Everybody opened their bags and started flexing. Throwing money into the air, holding gold bars to their ears and acting like they were phones calling each other. Los smiled at this. Everything was worth it to have this moment with his brothers.

"50 bandz and 2 gold bars, 50 ounces each. Gold is $2300 an ounce right now, y'all do the math. This is a starter kit, my niggas. Arizona is our new home. This Airbnb is good for another 28 days. Me and Lee up the road.

Juice, HP, I got a surgeon ready for y'all to choose different facial structures and shit. Then I got the pros with the CPNs ready for y'all too. Obviously y'all hot right now. Me and Boogie going tomorrow to choose ours. We all finna lay low for a minute. Get situated. Peezy, Kapone, I love y'all. Boog, you know what's up, brother," Los said and looked around the room.

"Wars aren't only fought in the field. Mental and emotional warfare is just as deadly and usually hurts more. Tugs at the heart strings, ya know?

We got the bricks ready. Lil Tony gon' show me the lay of the land. Once we situated, we gon' take this shit over. This gon' be a Mafia town. Any questions?" Los asked the room, after addressing them.

"Yeah! Where the hoes at?" Paris asked and threw a stack of hundreds in the air, making it rain blue faces in the basement.

"They everywhere, my boy!" Boogie said. "Bro got baby with' him though. He's finna be on lockdown! Especially after all that shit in the town! Niggas was going krazy!"

Los laughed. "Y'all niggas celebrate. We made it out alive. I'm finna be up the way. If y'all need me, hit me." He said and left them niggas in the basement to celebrate.

He went upstairs where Kaleah, Kayla, and Liv were drinking White Claws, talking about the niggas in the basement.

"Hey babe! You want one?" Kaleah offered him one. He declined.

"You ready, Lee?" he asked her, anxious to get her alone and spend some quality time together.

"Uhmmmm, yeah, brother. We coming too!" Liv said, talking about her and Kayla.

"Why don't y'all stay here with' the homies? Celebrate with' 'em?"

"Nigga please. I'm going with my sister. Come on," Liv said and started for the garage.

Kaleah and Kayla looked at them and started laughing, then followed Liv to the garage.

That bitch is a trip, Los thought, then headed that way too laughing.

***

Mario sat in the truck, looking at the GPS on his phone. His target hadn't moved all day. Unknown to Maria, Mario's side hustle was human trafficking. When he drove her car from the club on 190th to Happy Valley, he had gotten her address from the title in her glove box and left a GPS unit under the driver's seat.

He went to the apartment and found it empty. After knocking a few times with no answer, he picked the lock and let himself in. He went through her things, stealing her jewelry and anything else of value. In the top drawer behind the panties, he picked up a picture of her and a man.

He looked familiar. *Where do I know him from?* He put the picture in his pocket and left. When he got back to his apartment, he pulled the picture out again and studied it. Then it clicked for him!

He pulled up Telegram on his phone and scrolled up through the past month's messages and seen the picture of Los and the kill order for him!

He now knew Maria bumping into Eddy that night had to be more than just a coincidence. Especially since the very next night he was killed. He thought about messaging Bird, but decided not to. He was going to take initiative and snatch her ass up, see what she had to say. Then he'd let Bird know what he found out.

All that led him to where he was at now: Salem, Oregon. He was parked down the block from Maria's grandma's house. He sat behind tinted windows with her Audi in his view, waiting for the perfect moment. Years of kidnapping had taught him patience. This was going to move him up the ranks for sure. He might even become Mano De Jefe—hand of the boss— because of this.

***

"You have reached a number that has been disconnected."

"Fuck!" Maria screamed. She couldn't reach Los and was tired of sitting at her grandma's house. She looked at her call log and the many failed attempts at reaching Los and decided to go home. *Fuck it! And fuck him!* she thought.

She threw her suitcase in the trunk and was closing it when she felt a presence behind her.

She turned around and a pair of strong hands snatched her up and put a cloth over her mouth. She was unconscious seconds later.

Mario had to work fast, it was daylight on a busy residential street. He threw her body into the backseat of his Yukon, picked up her keys, got inside his truck, and drove off. He looked at her in the backseat, slumped. She had some explaining to do.

***

Maria came to slowly, tied to a chair in a dark basement. The last thing she remembered was putting her suitcase in the trunk, then nothing. She had a headache and her mouth was dry. She wanted to yell for help, but didn't want to alert her captors that she was awake. She fell back asleep...

SPLASH!

Cold water hit her in the face, waking her back up. Mario stood over her. "You got some explaining to do, chica," he told her.

She recognized him as the guy who drove her car from the club, the help.

"Oh my God," she said.

"No. God isn't here tonight. I decide who lives and dies tonight, mija," Mario spoke to her in a calm, confident voice.

She looked to the left and seen knives, pliers, a drill, and a mini blowtorch. She started sweating, fidgeting in her seat. Mario noticed all of this.

"Ahh. I see you've noticed the tools of my trade. I didn't rise up in La Familia because I'm soft. I'm also very creative with this shit," he said and winked at her. He picked up a filet knife and tossed it back and forth into his hands like a professional chef. "Who told you to go to the club that night, baby girl?" he asked her.

"Nobody did. It was Friday night and I wanted to go out. You've got the wrong girl. Whatever you think I did, I didn't do it," she pleaded with him.

"I'm going to ask you one more time," he said, "then I'm going to start peeling the skin off your fingers. Your man isn't coming to save you. He's in Arizona. He left you behind. Being loyal to him isn't going to get you out of here alive," he told her.

His statement hit a nerve with Maria. *Did he really leave me? After I risked my life for him? Did he shit on me again? After I fucked that fat fuck and brought him all the money?* she thought to herself. She said nothing to Mario.

He looked her up and down and said, "He's not coming for you. I respect how you move. You played your part perfectly the other night even when you fake dropped your purse and put this on the car." He held up the GPS for her. "Your skills could be put to use. With some training, in an organization like this, you could go very far, mija."

Maria sat there in deep thought, heartbroken again. *She wasn't going to die for this nigga. Especially after he used her again and changed his number without letting her know his new one.* She was tired of being the side bitch when she was out here doing main bitch shit for her man!

All that hurt and pain she was just feeling turned into bitterness within moments after learning his latest betrayal to her. *They say there's nothing like a woman scorned!*

"He left me?" she asked Mario.

"Si, mija. All can be forgiven if you join me," he said.

Maria knew deep down that this was ridiculous! *She didn't even know this man! And Los did tell her to stay out the way and not to leave her grandma's house! But fuck that! He left with another bitch! Again! He was going to feel her pain this time!* She looked up at Mario and said, "What do I gotta do?"

He looked at her and smiled. "I'm so glad you asked." Then walked up to her and used the knife to free her from bondage. "This is the plan..."

Chapter 21

Agent Lopez had stood at the top of the stairs to the basement and listened to Los' speech for a few minutes, while she was supposed to be using the bathroom. She was playing a dangerous game!

She heard enough to get a picture of what happened, what was going on now, and what was going to happen. She got a weird feeling that put her on alert every time Boogie looked at her, like he recognized her from somewhere. She brushed it off as him probably just wanting to fuck. She was committed to her job, but the longer she was around these people, the more she saw them as one big family that would do whatever to protect each other. She heard Los tell them to hit him if they needed him and walked back to the kitchen and resumed her role in the conversation. She felt right at home with Kaleah and her sister.

Raised by a single mom that worked all the time, she was home a lot by herself, lonely. So she embraced the sisterhood they were letting her into. *Would she be able to betray them? Or would she be able to betray the badge?* Only time would tell...

"Bitch, all them niggas down there single with a bag! You better bag one!" Kaleah was telling her sister when Kayla walked back in.

"Girl, them lil boys ain't ready. They wouldn't know what to do with all this!" Liv said, then ran her hands down her body and smacked herself on the ass.

All 3 started laughing at that.

"Kayla, girl you got to loosen up. Who you fucking with down there?" Liv questioned, all in her business.

"I don't know them like that to say. We'll see though. I'm more worried about this dry ass heat than all that!" Kayla said.

"Shit, I feel you," Kaleah agreed.

Los came up the stairs and into the kitchen. They left to the Airbnb Kaleah rented for them moments after that.

***

"Niggas been all over the news, brother. Y'all had the town going krazy!" Lil Tony said as him, Los, and Boogie drove down Camelback Street in Phoenix.

"Something like that," Los said, and all 3 of them started laughing at the nonchalant way he said it.

Lil Tony had picked them up from the Airbnb and taken them to see the surgeon. Now they were in traffic, getting familiar with the city.

"This is Camelback. You can find anything over here. It's wide open. It's kinda like everybody play this spot. Hoes, heats, work. Whatever you need you can get it around this bitch." They were at the red light on 27th and Camelback, by the KFC.

"Y'all niggas finna be good though. What the surgeon tell y'all?" Lil Tony asked.

"Shit, he want 10 bands for a new face. That aint too bad. He said he finna raise my cheeks up a lil and shave my jaw down. Fuck with my nose. I'll be a new person in 10 days," Los said.

"Oh, that's koo. Them CPNs got perfect credit scores too. Niggas can leave the lot in a Maybach fucking with me!" Lil Tony boasted. "Wifey been looking for a spot yet?"

"Nah, we at a muthafucking mansion Airbnb though. You got a plug on houses out here too, brother? Sheeesh, my nigga is tapped in!" Los said, proudly.

"Hell yeah! Boog, you been quiet back there? You good, Brody?" Lil Tony asked.

"Yeah, Bloody. Just thinking 'bout all this shit. It's like a paradise out here. I'm feeling AZ already!" Boogie told him.

"Hell muthafucking yeah, brother! You supposed to feel this way, my nigga," Lil Tony said as they pulled into Philobertos Taco spot.

"Now you know you them tacos in the town? Them small muthafuckas? A taco out here is a real deal taco, it's like 4 of them in one!" Lil Tony informed them as they walked in, placed their orders, and sat down.

"I got 20 bricks of raw, bro. Straight pow wow. I know you got motion out here by yo lonely, come fuck with yo Bros though. How much a whole chicken going for?" Los inquired.

"Shit, we can move 'em for 30 all day wholesale. It'd be better to have a trap jumping though. My shit is mobile. I'm busting juugs in traffic. I'm tapped in with these 79 Swan Blood niggas though out in Casa Grande. So it shouldn't be no problem buying one of they blocks. I'm a hit they big dawg and tell him we tryna chop it up," Lil Tony answered.

"Bet that," Los told him.

LATER THAT NIGHT

Pretty Please Nightclub

Scottsdale, Arizona

Earlier in the day, Lil Tony had hit the owner and gotten them a section in the VIP area. The whole team came out dipped in designer and dripped in buss down watches, chains, and earrings. It looked like the Phoenix Suns was in the building. For Kaleah, it was a much-needed break from being cooped up in the house since being shot. For Los, it was a chance to network and put together some much-needed plays. Blue bottles of Bel-Aire Rosé in ice buckets were at every table in the section, along with bottles of 1942

Don Julio and Clase Azul—the tequila bottle with the bell on top. They were lit, having a stress-free, drama-free night.

Lil Tony tapped Los on the shoulder and said, "They just got here. I told 'em slide to the section."

"Yup, it's good," Los said and stood up. He told Kaleah, "I'm a move to this table over here, baby. I gotta holla at this nigga right quick." He assured her. He was concerned about her being around people she didn't know and having PTSD about it. He motioned for Lil Tony to come and sit with him.

Two niggas walked up, flamed up in all red, gang banging. One was short, bald-headed, with a beard and glasses on. The other was tall with long hair. Both had tats on their necks and faces. The short one looked familiar. When he got closer and seen who he was meeting up with, he said, "My nigga Los! What's good! What you doing out here?" His name was Brazo. They had done time together.

"My nigga!" Los said and embraced him. "This the nigga you talking 'bout?" Los said to Lil Tony. "This is bro. But what's up though? I got that raw at a good price. What y'all tryna do? You the man to see about it?" Los said to Brazo.

"Man, something like that. You got that raw, you said? What's the ticket?" Brazo asked.

"This what I was thinking, bro. I slide you 3 joints for free, and 100K. Let me buy one of the blocks in y'all hood?" Los said, ready to negotiate.

"You want one of my blocks? 3 joints?" Brazo asked.

"Yeah... After you get rid of them, come re-up with me. I'll lock you in at 20 for the whole birdy."

"Bet that. Keep the 100 bandz though, Blood. We under the Red Flag, you feel me. Welcome to AZ!" Brazo shouted the last part and they shook on it, locking it in.

Los grabbed 2 bottles of Bel-Aire and handed 1 to Brazo. "I'm a drop them off to you tomorrow, my nigga."

"Yup. We gon' link up. I'm a show you yo new trap," Brazo told him. They tapped the bottles and took a big ass swig of them.

Los went back to Kaleah after introducing Brazo and Ratchet to the team.

"You good, babe?" Kaleah asked him.

"Yeah, Lee. Things coming together perfectly," he told her.

Kayla sat back with a flute of champagne in her hand, relaxed, enjoying herself. She was buzzing from the alcohol and noticed Boogie looking at her. He slid up on her.

"You enjoying yo night?" he asked her.

"Yeah, I like it. You enjoying yourself tonight?" she said back.

"Of course. These last few days been hectic. I'm alive though, so I can't complain."

He raised the drink in his hand and tapped it against hers. "To new beginnings, new money, and new friendships." He said that last part looking into her eyes.

"You got an exotic look to you. I'm positive I've never seen you before, but you feel so familiar, you feel me?"

"Yeah, I know what you mean," she agreed with him. She wanted to press him further about these hectic days he was talking about but decided not to.

"You plan on staying out here?" he asked.

"I don't know yet, why? What about you?"

"Kuz if you are, I'm definitely tryna spend some time with you... Shit, even if you leaving, I'm tryna kick it. I fuck with yo laid back, observant energy," he told her.

Kaleah poked Los in the ribs and pointed at Boogie putting Kayla's number in his phone.

"My bro 'bout to fuck yo homegirl. Shiiit, if she go to the house with him, she might get hit by the team!" Los joked.

"You're sick," Kaleah said and laughed. She put her hand underneath the table and started massaging his pipe through his jeans. "I'm tryna get fucked tonight toooo," she whispered in his ear, drawing out the word, licking his neck.

Los put his hand underneath the table also and moved it between her thighs and up. She wasn't wearing any panties.

"Huuunh," she inhaled as he put his fingers into her and moved them in and out, while moving his thumb in a circular motion on her clit. This had him rock hard.

"Oooh baby, I'm 'bout to cum... Don't stop," she whispered in his ear, looking around, making sure nobody noticed them.

She came all over his fingers, took them out, and sucked the juices off at the table. *Fuck it!*

Los tapped Boogie, "Bro, I'm 'bout to dip. You good?"

"Yup. I'm finna spend the night with ol' girl at y'all spot," Boogie said.

"Okay, brother!" Kaleah said and went to dap him up. "I'ma tell my girl to take it easy on you!" she joked.

"Jokes!" Boogie said and dapped her up, laughing his ass off with her.

Kayla sat back and watched this. Not as Special Agent Lopez but as Kayla Lopez; the girl who's been searching for the closeness of family all her life...

Chapter 22

"So this is it. Yo new trap," Brazo said to Los as he walked with him down the block in West Casa Grande, introducing him to the people outside that lived and worked there.

"Don't look too jumping to me," Los told him.

"Give it a few hours. It's early, ma boy. This is AZ. Don't shit pop off during the day like that. These smokers would die of dehydration! Y'all finna cook up though? Or just soft?" Brazo inquired.

"Both. This shit finna be like a New York block in the eighties, ma boy!" Los said, as they walked up the porch steps to the trap house.

"So this is it. This spot does a hunnid a week. With that shit y'all brought up here, y'all should triple that in no time. I got the plug on the fetty powder too. You fucking with it?" Brazo asked him.

"Word? Let me think about it. I'll let you know, Blood. Them fetty smokers a different breed of junkie. Back home I had it Brackin with the 30's but shit, we gon' take it one thing at a time, you feel me," Los told him.

"On dead homies. That shit like crack in the eighties!" Brazo said and started laughing at his own joke. "Y'all niggas stay strapped though. It goes without saying that since y'all in the hood, y'all gon' have to ride for the hood too. I'm not talking 'bout going on missions an' shit. But if niggas come through here tripping, y'all gotta shut that shit down, Blood."

Aint no question, Bloody. You know how my niggas give it up. Any friend of mine, we gon' share the same enemies, Los said back, assuring him.

"Say less then, my nigga," Brazo said, extending his hand for Los to shake.

Los shook it, throwing up the B with their fingers as they did it. Locked in.

***

Lee Lee was slowly regaining full motion of her shoulder after almost 3 months of physical therapy.

Her and Liv decided to open an upscale hair salon in Casa Grande, catering to all the career housewives in the area. It was also a profitable way to wash all the drug money Los was making.

Los had recovered from the facial surgery nicely. When he took the bandages off a week after and the swelling was down, Kaleah was shocked at how she didn't recognize him. She eventually warmed up to it. Boogie, Juice, and HP all had their faces and fingerprints worked on also and had recovered.

Boogie had been staying at the new house with them, sleeping in Kayla's room. They were getting along just fine. Boogie could feel that she was holding something back. But shit, he wasn't looking for love, and assumed that she wasn't either. They were all living in the moment.

***

Agent Malone called Lopez and got her voicemail again. He was frustrated and worried about her lack of communication with him. He understood she was deep undercover, but this was getting ridiculous.

He booked a flight to Arizona. He would investigate her lack of contact in person and go from there.

He touched down in Phoenix the next night. It was fall in Portland. He hadn't thought of the climate difference, so he almost had a heat stroke when he stepped outside. He got into his rental car and turned the AC up immediately.

Ahhhh, much better! he thought.

He dialed Lopez and was surprised when the phone actually rang this time, indicating it was on.

"Well hello, stranger," he said when she answered.

"Hey. I can't speak for long," she whispered. "But I'm making very little progress. It's like with the move from Oregon, they've went completely legit."

"Well, I'm leaving Phoenix, driving down I-10 right now. I'll be in Casa Grande in 20 minutes. So you can tell me over lunch. Or you can come back to Portland and debrief there," Malone said.

"Fuck. Okay. Meet me at Chili's right off the freeway in an hour," Lopez answered.

"Roger that," Malone said and hung up.

***

"Who was that?" Boogie asked her suspiciously, after catching her whispering into the phone, looking guilty.

"Oh, that was just my uncle back in Sacramento. I was rushing him off the phone because he's always hitting me up for money," Kayla answered him.

"Yeah, okay," he said, dropping the subject. Not bringing up why she was speaking on a cheap Android instead of her iPhone.

"But hey, I'm going to the store. Do you need anything?" she asked him.

"Yeah. Grab a gallon of Hennessy XO, and a case of waters."

"Got you, baby," she said and kissed him on his lips and left.

***

Now Boogie didn't care one way or another if the bitch was fucking with a nigga from out there, but he did care about her pillow talking and becoming a liability to the team. So he waited 'til she was out of the gate to hop in his car and follow her.

He trailed a football field behind her at all times. He knew for certain she was doing more than just "going to the store" like she said when she passed hella grocery stores and corner markets during the drive.

She pulled into the Chili's parking lot and got out of her car. Instead of going into the restaurant, she got into a black SUV with rear tinted windows. He took pictures of her meeting with an older white man.

He parked in the strip mall parking lot next to the restaurant. There was no doubt in his mind who the uppity white man in the suit was—he was them people for sure!

***

"What are you doing out here, Malone? You're risking my cover! Not to mention my life," Lopez said immediately after entering the car.

"I haven't heard from you in months, Lopez. What the fuck do you mean 'what am I doing out here'?" he said back to her. "I'm this close to pulling you back to fucking Portland! This fucking close!" He held up his fingers, showing her how close he really was.

Unknown to them, Boogie was 50 yards away, watching this whole scene go down while on the phone with Los, getting instructions.

"I just need more time. I honestly have not seen anything indicating them continuing to operate their criminal activities, or them starting anything new," she lied to

Malone, choosing her new family over the badge she used to love.

***

"Blood, I'm telling you, she's in the car with the fucking boys right now!" Boogie told Los.

"Yeah, he looks like the police fasho," Los said to Boogie over speakerphone, looking at the pictures of Kayla in the car with the white man. "Come back here though before she does and act like everything is good."

"I got you, brother. I can't believe I been giving this police ass bitch this dick!" Boogie said and started laughing.

Los laughed with him. "I'ma handle this the right way, bro. Can't jump the gun in a situation like this. Especially if she's a fucking undercover. This gon' break Lee Lee's heart."

Unknown to Los, Kaleah was standing at the top of the balcony, overlooking the living room when she heard them say Kayla's name. She stopped and listened to the conversation.

Kayla was the police? This whole time? She knew what she had to do. She brought this snake-ass bitch around, so she would be the one to get rid of her. She turned around and headed for Liv's room. They had to figure this out ASAP. Wasn't no way in hell she was letting this bitch send her nigga and his brothers to jail, ripping their family apart.

Later That Night

The light from the fridge was the only illumination in the kitchen. Kayla had awoken at 4 AM and had a craving for cold orange juice.

"I'm gonna give you one chance to tell the truth."

She jumped, dropping the orange juice, spilling it everywhere, surprised at the voice in the room with her. She thought she was alone.

"Oh, hey Los. What are you doing down here in the dark?" she asked him.

"Like I said. I'll give you one time to be honest with me." After he said this, he slid his phone across the marble countertop. It stopped in front of her, showing a picture of her and Malone in the car, talking.

"I told Lee it was something off about you, but she said I was just paranoid. But you're the police, aren't you?" he asked her calmly, in full control of his emotions and the situation.

"What is this? You're having me followed?" Kayla said to him, searching for an out.

"Nah, I didn't have to. Let me ask you this though. Do you truly got love for Kaleah? Or was she just a decoy? A pawn in this game we playing?"

"No... I truly love Lee. I've come to love all of you..." she answered.

"These past few months you've seen us share love and loyalty. We've made you part of our family. So are you more loyal to the badge that will never love you back, or are you more loyal to the family we've made you part of?"

She didn't even have to think about her answer, she told him instantly and truthfully, "I'm loyal to this family. I love this family." She said and dropped a few tears. This was everything she craved growing up.

Los seen this and nodded his head. "So what are you? FBI? DEA? ATF?"

"I'm with the FBI. I told my partner today that I had nothing to report. I've been out of contact the last 4 months we've been out here. Believe me when I say, I would do nothing to destroy this."

"FBI huh? That's wild. Appreciate your honesty. I'ma keep this to myself. You gon' have to apologize to Boog though. From now on, you're my eyes and ears in the FBI. You gon' have to prove your loyalty to this family though." Los told her.

"I can be that for you, Los. And what is it you need me to do to prove my love and loyalty?"

"I need you to destroy the file you guys have on me and anything y'all have on my team. Then I need you to kill your partner..."

"I got you...." Kayla answered.

"Bet that. Go get some sleep," Los told her. "We've got some long days ahead of us."

Chapter 23

Kayla walked into the federal building in Phoenix nervously. Lying to Malone was easy; that was only verbal. This was an action, something physical. Surprisingly to her though, this wasn't too hard.

Her being distant from the Bureau these past few months that she was undercover had helped her with this decision. It was safe to say she loved her new life. Even more surprising to her was how well her conversation with Boogie went.

"So you're the FBI, huh... weird-ass bitch," he said to her, shaking his head in disappointment. He had spoke with Los about this very thing earlier in the day though, so he knew to play it cool with her. He truly meant his first sentence though...

"Please, Ace... let me explain..." Kayla pleaded. She was shocked at how much she felt for him.

"Explain what? How you was plotting to arrest me?"

"Baby, no," she said, and reached out for his arm. "I told my partner there was nothing new to report. That life is over for me. I'm part of the family foreal. I love you guys foreal."

"Yeah, okay. You definitely finna have yo chance to show yo love. It's actually yo time to shine right now. You ready to go?" he asked her.

"Been ready, Daddy. Now let me show you my love," she answered. All that led up to this moment.

She walked into the room where the out-of-town Agents used the computers. She sat down at the desk, logged in with another Agent's passcode, and looked up the Carlos Mills

MAFIA file. She wasn't worried about the cameras—she was wearing a wig and turned her face down whenever she passed one. She was shocked at some of the stuff she was reading. She also felt pride in her chest at how smart they moved and how they had managed to stay lowkey until recently. She clicked on the home button, and her hand hovered over the delete option. After this, there was no going back.

Fuck it... I'm all in, she thought, and clicked down, and the file was officially gone from the Bureau database. Now all she had left to do was knock down Malone—a street-savvy FBI veteran...

Her and Boogie booked seats on a Southwest Airlines flight back to Portland to accomplish this task.

They got there, and a black 750i Beamer with black tints from Turo was waiting for them in the arrival section. They got in, and Boogie dropped her off at the hotel while he went and handled a few things. He picked her up when it was dark outside, and she got in, ready to commit a murder with her man. She loved it! She never once thought or felt that she might be in over her head.

"What kinda car you said he was in?" Boogie asked as they pulled up to a house in Northeast Portland's Parkrose district.

"The black Charger should be parked outside of his house," she said as they pulled up to Malone's home. His car wasn't there.

"Well, he's not here. So where to next?" Boogie inquired.

"Let's check the bar on 125th and Sandy—The Wooden Chicken. He usually be up in there on nights he's off and plays pool. He likes to say 'he's checking the temperature of the city.' So he goes to hood spots."

A few minutes later, they pulled up to 125th and seen the black Charger parked outside. "Bingo," Boogie said, and parked the car on the street side with a view of the Charger, waiting for him to step outside.

Boogie handed her a Ghost Glock. That was one of the errands Los had sent him on—to stop at Kobe's spot and pick up Los' package of Polymer Ghost Glocks and threaded suppressors. This was one mission where errors were not to be made.

She took the gun from him and racked the slide, putting one up top, then screwed the suppressor onto it. She pulled her ski mask down her face. Now all they had left to do was wait.

Thirty minutes later, Malone walked out with a female.

"Babe, he has company... what should I do?" Kayla asked Boogie, concerned about killing his companion, a civilian.

"No witnesses... now go handle yo business," he told her.

Kayla eased out of the car and crept across the street with the gun leading her way. She heard Malone's voice, telling his companion the plans he had for her tonight. Unfortunately, those plans were about to be cancelled.

Kayla crept up behind him just as he sat down into the car and shot him four times—*PFFT! PFFT! PFFT! PFFT!*—all in the neck and face.

The girl with him started screaming, so she shot her in the face also—*PFFT! PFFT! PFFT! PFFT!*

The gun was silenced, so besides the screaming, the whole thing was quiet and took about 20 seconds. She closed both of their doors, so hopefully nobody would find them 'til at least tomorrow.

She ran back to the Beamer and got in. Boogie sped off. She was truly forgiven and an official member of the family in his eyes.

Nayarit, Mexico

Maria wiped the sweat from her face with the terry cloth towel and threw it to the side. It was noon and she was outside working with her trainer, ex-UFC star Tito Ortiz, on hand-to-hand combat. Later in the day, she would work on her shooting.

It had been two months since Mario had snatched her up on that West Salem Street. She loved the feeling of watching her body transform due to her strict diet and daily training program. She also loved hitting her target every time she trained with the guns on the ranch. She was a completely new woman. A machine. *A machine intent on revenge.*

Mario had introduced her to Bird. He was actually thankful she had lined up his snitching ass brother. Instead of their relationship becoming sexual, they became close like siblings, and there was nothing she wouldn't do for her *Carnal.* And he was teaching her all about the Cartel and what it took to run it.

"Ugghh!" she screamed out as she delivered a hard-hitting five-piece, ending it with a jump kick. Her trainer was amazed at her progress.

"Wow. I didn't see that coming. Great work, Maria," he said to her.

"Thank you," she said, panting, only slightly out of breath.

She walked over to the gazebo and took a drink of water and picked up her phone. She had a notification from Juan. She had been keeping up with Los' activities in Arizona as much as she could. He had sent her a copy of the marriage certificate Kaleah Bay had purchased at the Casa Grande courthouse.

This had her seething! Even though she was essentially an enemy of Los, she still wished it was her marrying him and starting a family. *It looked like she had a wedding to crash!*

***

Kaleah, Liv, and Kayla were at the boutique getting their dresses fitted.

"So where were you and Ace off to these last few days?" Kaleah asked Kayla.

"He had a couple of loose ends to take care of in Portland, so I went with him," she answered.

"Oh yeah? Y'all getting serious?" she inquired.

"I mean that's my nigga. You know what? I aint even gon' hold you. I love that man. All this trying on dresses and wedding planning got me thinking about marriage too," Kayla said.

If you live that long, Liv thought but said, "Shit, I'm a player for life!" And they all started laughing.

"Well girl, make sure that nigga feels the same way as you before you start buying rings," Kaleah told Kayla.

Kayla looked at both of them before she said this: "Bitch, my period is late. It was supposed to come two weeks ago. I'm too scared to take a test though. I would literally die if he didn't want my baby..."

"Ace is a stand-up guy when it comes to his children. I'm sure he'll want you to keep it. Let's grab a test on the way home."

Kaleah shot Liv a look after she said this. *This pregnancy complicates our plans.*

***

"It went smooth like that?" Los said after Boogie told him about the hit in Portland. "I'm telling you, brother, she was ice cold. No hesitation. She good in my eyes. She might've started out with a hidden agenda, but she solid now. She for the team all the way," Boogie said to Los.

"That's good to hear. No cap, I thought about killing the bitch. But that would've brought us way too much heat. Plus, she's more useful to us alive. She good in my book, brother."

Los said the words Boogie wanted to hear. He was ready to plead her case if Los would've said otherwise. He was falling in love.

***

On the way home they grabbed a few pregnancy tests, and after they got home, Kaleah pissed on one too for the fuck of it and was shocked at the outcome... she was pregnant.

Kayla came running into the room happy with her results and seen the look on Kaleah's face. "What's wrong?" she asked her. Then seen the positive test on the bathroom counter. "Yes bitch! We're having babies at the same time!" Kayla yelled, then hugged her.

Kaleah was happy, but speechless. She couldn't wait to tell Los.

Chapter 24

Officer Borlee read the police report for Malone's murder and shook his head. Portland was turning into a warzone. Not too many gangs had the balls to murder an FBI agent. He assumed it was the same people that killed his officers at Kenton Park. The same ones that killed a state trooper.

None of his informants had heard a thing on any of the Mafia members lately. After Delon and Chris had murdered the state trooper, things had quieted down in the city after that night. He couldn't wait to catch Carlos also and take a look at those hand tattoos. He was patient though. He was certain that day would come, and when it did, he would be ready for it.

***

"You failed. Miserably I might add. Do you remember the price I said you would pay for that failure?" Bird said to Marky over FaceTime.

"I got yo money right here. I just need more time. Los is a slippery muthafucka. But I'll catch him. What were the chances of him hitting the spot the same time I was going in to re-up? That shouldn't count as a strike against the gang," Marky told him.

"You're lucky I'm in a good mood. I happen to know Los is currently somewhere in the Phoenix metro area. His bitch just purchased a marriage certificate in Casa Grande, but the trail runs dry after that. Fly your hitters in and see what you can dig up. I'll send the address for your re-up too," Bird said, then ended the call. Good help was hard to find these days.

***

"Let me a get a 1942 with pineapple juice," Los said to the waiter.

"I'll take a water with lemon in it," Kaleah ordered.

"Why you not drinking, babe?" Los asked her.

"Just not in the mood. Plus it's hot in here. I rather have water after that meal we just ate," she answered.

"That shit was fire, huh? They need to hurry up with this cheesecake though."

Just as he said that, the waiter appeared with a slice for each of them.

Los noticed something sticking out of his. "What the fuck is this?" He was getting ready to trip on the waiter! He pulled out the positive pregnancy test. "Whoooaa," he said.

"Congratulations, baby! You're about to be a daddy!" Kaleah exclaimed.

"Word?" Los said with the test in his hand. "That's why you not drinking, babe?" he asked her.

"Yes, babe. I'm pregnant..."

"Dead homies! We having a baby then!" he yelled in the restaurant. People at the tables close to them started to clap for them and congratulate the young couple.

"How long have you known?" he asked her.

"Just yesterday. Kayla is too. She's sure it's Boogie's," she told him.

"Bro bout to be happy as me! Just know, Lee, I'm with you and I got our family forever," Los told her and leaned over the table and kissed her on the lips. "I'm glad she's pregnant at the same time as you though. Boog been homesick. This gives him a purpose out here, something to grind for. Plus that's sis now. She's part of this family fasho fasho."

***

Later that night Kaleah was in Liv's room getting her hair braided. "We can't kill her, sis. She's pregnant. I won't have that karma coming my way now that I'm pregnant also. I think she did more than just go to Portland to keep Ace company. There's more to the story. Los called her sis today. And said she's part of the family. And I know for sure he doesn't say shit like that lightly," Kaleah said.

"Well, sis, I'm a keep my eyes on her. First time she slips that's her ass though," Liv said back to her.

"Straight the fuck up, sister. 'til then though we gon' give her the benefit of the doubt."

Chapter 25

"Without the witnesses to testify on an already weak case, I can't justify leaving this prisoner in custody, prosecutor," the judge said at Caesar's hearing for pre-trial release pending his new trial.

"With all due respect, judge, I think we know what happened to the witnesses or should I say who happened to the witnesses," the prosecutor said angrily.

"Objection, Your Honor. Those witnesses were relocated by the U.S. Marshals and that's a secret process only them and the Attorney General know about. Unless it's them they're referring to when he says 'who,' it's not my client's fault those shady people met a shady end. The defense moves for not only pre-trial today but a complete dismissal of all charges against my client. If it pleases the court, Your Honor," Caesar's high-paid defense attorney spoke.

Caesar was sitting at the defense table, confident that he was going home today. He looked behind him and winked at Dolce. He couldn't have done this without her. He planned to show his appreciation for the rest of their lives. He was the new Jefe of The Organization and planned to bring his Cartel to new heights with her at his side. He also planned on going to Arizona and meeting Los in person. He was very grateful for that young man and his fearless actions.

"You'll be out tonight," his lawyer whispered to him.

"My man," Caesar said and stuck out his hand for his lawyer to shake. Getting out of jail was one of the best feelings in the world.

"I'll be at the gate waiting for you, baby," Dolce told him as he was being led back out of the courtroom.

***

Caesar and Dolce chartered a private jet and flew to Phoenix the same night he was released. They had a villa in Scottsdale that they owned through a shell corporation. They planned to relax and enjoy each other the first night and get right to business tomorrow. They had a lot of catching up to do, the sexual tension was high.

He had texted Los the address and told him to come to the villa at 2 p.m.

As always, Los was prompt.

"My man Caesar. It's nice to finally meet you. I've heard nothing but great things," Los told him after he sat down to the lunch Dolce had prepared for them.

"Los, the pleasure is mine. I can't thank you enough for the work you put in. Your actions lead to today. Understand there is none of this without you," Caesar said and lifted his drank up to Los. "As a token of my appreciation, I want to welcome you and your team into my Organization."

Los lifted his glass in respect back to the Jefe and knew this was one of the biggest moments of his life. The game changer. He was really putting on for his squad.

"As another token of my appreciation, I have my lawyers on Cream's case, and we plan to have bro home by this time next year also." Caesar knew there was no one without the other.

"I appreciate you man, foreal. That shit mean a lot to me. I hate to leave my family in that muthafucka," Los said. "I got my team out here with me. We got shit booming. I know with you out now we can take it to the next level. I came out here with 20 bricks. We at the last few right now."

"I see. Well I can definitely help you with a fresh supply whenever you need it. I'll have 100 joints dropped off to you tomorrow. Bring me a million point five back," Caesar said to the young hustler.

Los couldn't have wished for a better price. He didn't wanna sound too excited, like a nerd. "Sounds good to me," he said, in control of his emotions.

"And take my word for it, the quality of my product is superior to anything out right now," Caesar assured him.

"I'm definitely loving the sound of that," Los told him, rubbing his hands together like Birdman, thinking of the multi-million dollar profit his team was about to make with their first flip.

"How you loving yo freedom though? This spot nice as hell," Los said.

"It's a blessing, brother. This is one of many properties we own in many different states and countries. Real estate is the best laundry mat around. When you ready to look at some properties, let me know. We all at our own levels individually, but being part of the Organization, we aim to rise collectively. This is a hate-free zone. A sucka-free zone. We share success over here. I'm the Jefe, don't get that misunderstood. I earned my spot. But don't think of me as your boss, but as your partner. We all serve a purpose. We all excel at different things so everything you need is in-house. Supply and demand. We never have to go to an outsider for anything. All the money stays home that way," Caesar said to Los, kicking knowledge and letting Los know what was really going on.

"I feel the fuck outta that," Los responded, impressed. "When my money right, I'm a tap in bout a few things you just said. But don't hesitate to call me for anything. You know what's up with my guys. I got young, hungry wolves with me. Coming out here was a change that was necessary but we've adapted and took over our surroundings. If you not too busy, you tryna slide by the trap with me?" Los asked, checking Caesar's heart.

"No doubt. Let me go change and we can leave in 10 minutes. You drive," Caesar said then stood up and walked into the house to get dressed.

***

"Yo Loso, we only got one chicken left. I got our master chef cooking it up in the lab right now," Boogie said to Los when he walked in, not noticing Caesar. Their tradition was to always cook up the last bird and hand-to-hand it for the biggest flip possible.

"That's good shit. I'ma have the packs for niggas tomorrow. Boog, this Caesar. Who we slid on them Mexicans in Woodburn for. He just came home yesterday," Los told him, introducing Caesar.

"Caesar, welcome home. Them cages aint for no one. I'm Boogie," he said, introducing himself to the Jefe.

"Nice to meet you, Boogie. I appreciate you taking care of that for me. Like I told Los, welcome to The Organization. If it's anything I can do, I got y'all," Caesar said to him.

"This way," Los told Caesar, walking into the kitchen where the OG dope smoker was sitting at the table testing out the new batch that HP was cooking up. His eyes rolled into the back of his head in bliss as he hit the straight shooter. HP was definitely him in the kitchen.

Los waited to introduce the guest, never saying too much in front of a dope feind. "My nigga. It's time to go," Los said, shaking the smoker back into reality. He tossed him 5 dubs. "Go poof these with the smokers on the block. Let 'em know we open," he instructed him.

"Like I said though, brother. This is Caesar. The Jefe," Los said respectfully after the smoker left.

"Yeah boy. We major league now," HP said, and shook 'em both up. "Welcome to my laboratory. I cook all the packs myself. My pops was a old dope smoker. This an old school recipe he got in LA in the 80's. He say he got it from Freeway Ricky. But pops be capping," he started to joke.

"I see, I see. This a nice setup y'all got going on. Can you handle 100 packs though?" Caesar tested him.

"Can I? Shiiit, if I had 100 joints I'd make every nigga in this house a millionaire by next week!" HP boasted.

Caesar liked what he was seeing and what he was hearing. This was an efficient, profitable operation ready to go to the next level. He would help take them there.

"We run this shit in shifts. Keeps everybody sharp and keeps everybody part of the work and reward, you feel me?" Los said to Caesar. "The other homies at they spot right now, getting they rest. I promote healthy eating and healthy living. The niggas around me gotta have some goals and game about they self. No nerd niggas allowed. We pop out at the clubs and let these bitches and niggas know who run this shit every now and then. Shit, it's Friday. You tryna pop out tonight? I can get a section at Zumas in Tempe for tonight. No problem," Los asked Caesar after preaching to him.

"I'm down. I'ma bring Dolce with me," Caesar responded.

"Yup, I'ma bring my bitch with me too. That's how I stunt on these niggas. With my bad ass, unapproachable bitch they could never have, you feel me?" Los said to him.

"Indeed I do," Caesar agreed with him.

Chapter 26

Zumas Night Club
Tempe, Arizona

The DJ played Lil Blood's *Get It In* featuring Yatta, and the club went crazy. Los had brought the whole team out to show Caesar and Dolce love tonight. They had two sections connected next to each other for the welcome home party.

True to his word, Los brought LeeLee out to shit on every other bitch there. She had on a black dress with rips down the sides that she made herself, Louis Vuitton knee-high boots, and a diamond tennis chain necklace with a pendant that spelled out *LEELEE*. Dolce didn't disappoint either. He made a mental note to introduce the two later on in the night. There were bottles of 1942 and Belaire Rosé everywhere. Kaleah and Kayla sipped on sparkling water.

"This spot is jumping," Caesar said to Los. "Appreciate the invite."

"Wait for it," Los told him. As he said this, the DJ spoke after the song ended.

"Showing love tonight to the Big Boss who just came home! My man *King Caesar!*" he shouted into the mic.

Caesar stood up, walked to the edge of the section, and looked down at the crowd. He took out a knot of hundreds, undid the rubber band, and threw it into the air—making it rain 200 one-hundred-dollar bills onto the crowd. The club went *insane*. The DJ put on Celly Ru's *All Blues*.

After Caesar sat back down, Dolce danced her way over and sat herself in his lap. “Hey papi. How’re you feeling tonight?” she asked him.

“This is definitely a night to remember. We gotta take Los and Kaleah to the clubs in Spain,” he told her.

“I’m glad you’re enjoying yourself. *Welcome home*, baby! I can’t quit saying that. I’m so happy you’re here with me. With you home and your brother gone, The Organization can finally come into the new era. Your brother was holding us back.”

That conversation went on while Los and LeeLee were having their own, ten feet away.

“I wanna take advantage of every opportunity with you, baby, and truly grow together. You my child’s mother. I wanna see you win just as bad as I wanna see me win,” Los told her.

“Vice versa, baby. I just wanna grow with you and grow old with you,” LeeLee said back to him.

“I was talking to Caesar earlier and he opening my eyes to other opportunities. This is a great move for the team. Them long nights led to these moments.”

“Baby Daddy, if I didn’t know any better I’d say you kicking game to me right now,” she said playfully, and kissed him. He stood up and told her to follow him.

“It’s somebody I gotta introduce you to,” he said, walking over to Caesar and Dolce.

“Dolce, this my fiancée Kaleah. Kaleah, this my man’s wife, Dolce,” Los introduced the two women. She had met Caesar when they first arrived at the club. The ladies sat down with each other and instantly clicked. With two bad, alpha bitches, you never know—either they going to hate each other or love each other.

Los sat down next to Caesar, raised his glass and said, “To new partnerships and new money.” They tapped glasses and took a sip.

"So what are your plans? You staying out here?" Los inquired.

"For the next few days, then going to my estate in California and onto Mexico to officially be crowned King by the Four Families. You'll have my direct line though. My phone is available to you at any time," Caesar assured him.

"Appreciate the love. Watch what I do with it, my boy."

At the same time Los and Caesar were having this conversation, two niggas were plotting on them from across the room.

"That nigga threw at least 20k in the crowd and his neck is bussing. He looking like a sweet lick to me. What you think, cuzz?" Stink Locc asked his homeboy.

"On Hood. He don't look too tough to me. His bitch got at least 100k on her neck and finger. I *neeeed* that," G Locc said, agreeing.

"Say less. It's bout 3 a.m. right now. This club finna close in an hour. On Hood—when they come out, we on 'em," Stink Locc said.

"What about they potnas?" G Locc asked.

"Shit, we can really get on them outta town slob niggas too if they in the way. Word to my dead homies, cuzz," Stink Locc answered.

***

"Where y'all park at?" Los asked Caesar, exiting the club with his baby mom and his team next to him.

"Around the corner. We'll be good. Hit me anytime. I'll have those dropped off to you in the morning," Caesar told him.

"Bet. I'ma get with you," Los said, then walked off in the opposite direction.

Caesar and Dolce hit the corner and were ten feet from the GT Maserati when Stink and G Locc popped out from behind a port-a-potty, toting Baby A's, barefaced.

"Keep yo mouth closed and hand it all over, cuzz," Stink said to them.

"My G, do you know who you robbing tonight?" Caesar asked, moving his body in front of Dolce.

"Nigga, what? I don't give a fuck if you knew El Chapo, nigga. I said gimme all that," Stink Locc spat.

Dolce had a Glock 43 under her dress and was attempting to grab it after Caesar stepped in front of her.

"Ah ah ah. Leave yo hands where I can see them, baby," G said, walking up on her with the rifle pointed up at her. She put her hands up.

"You heard what the DJ said. *King Caesar*, you bums. Remember that name—it's gonna change your life," Caesar said venomously.

Stink Locc smacked him in the face with the stock of the Baby A and he fell. He put the rifle in his face, grinding him in the eye with it.

G stuck the barrel of the gun in Dolce's ribs.

"Don't try anything stupid, mamacita," he told her.

Stink reached down, snatched the diamond Cuban off Caesar's neck, and ran his pockets—coming out with a knot of blue hundreds.

"It could've been this easy. But you had to be hard for your bitch," Stink Locc said, then snatched the diamond choker and ring from Dolce and pocketed them.

"You can keep this," he said, dropping the Maserati fob on Caesar's chest.

"I seen you tryna reach for something. Don't think I didn't have my eyes on you too, bitch. What you got down here?" he spat at Dolce, reached under her dress, took the compact 9mm from her thigh holster, rubbing his finger across her bare pussy lips as he did.

"Wouldn't wanna leave you with this and you make a mistake you might not come back from." He racked the slide and caught the shell, then dropped the magazine and threw it on top of the building they were next to. He tossed the empty gun at her feet and said, "Now y'all have a good night."

She looked back at him with hate in her eyes. "Just remember that name—*King Caesar*." Then Stink and G ran off into the night.

Dolce ran to Caesar and helped him up. "Baby, are you okay?" she asked, concerned.

"Yeah, I'm good. Those *putos* don't know what the fuck they just did," he said calmly. "Get in the car. I'm calling Los. He can't be too far."

They got in the Maserati and Caesar had Los on the phone.

"My boy, have you left the area yet?" he asked.

"Nah, we posted around the block. Why, what's good?"

"These clowns from the club just robbed us at gunpoint. Pull up on me ASAP."

Los was pissed when he heard this. This happened on *his watch*.

"I'm on the way right now," Los said, hopping in his car and telling his team to follow him.

He pulled up and Caesar hopped out the Masi and met Los in the street.

"Y'all good, my nigga?" Los asked.

Caesar nodded. "Yo man owns this club, correct?"

"Yeah. What you thinking?" Los answered.

Caesar pointed to the cameras on the side of the club. "They weren't wearing masks. Hit him for the tape. Pay whatever it costs and meet me at my villa," he said.

"I'm on it ASAP," Los said, already scrolling through his contacts.

They embraced and Caesar left the scene.

Los walked over to the Cadillac EXT that Boogie was driving, with Juice and HP riding with him. Kapone and Paris were at the trap holding it down.

"Some clown niggas just robbed Caesar and his lady. I just text Bone to call me ASAP. We finna get that tape, find these niggas, and set a demo—let niggas know this shit not sweet," he told them.

"Damn. Niggas robbed a muthafucking cartel leader and didn't even know it," Juice said, shaking his head. "Dumb ass dead niggas."

DING!

"This Bone right now," Los said, reading the text. "I'm finna go in and grab that tape. It might be a long night."

***

Los dropped off LeeLee, Kayla, and Liv. He told Boogie to ride with him out to Caesar's villa in Scottsdale.

They got there with the tape and Caesar was waiting for them. He let them in and they went straight to the living room where Caesar had a bottle of Casa Migos Reposado open already. He told them to help themselves after he made himself a drink.

"So, the video is clear?" he asked Los. "'Cause this can't go unpunished," he said to them. Los handed him the phone so he could see for himself. "You can hear them niggas clearly saying *cuzz* to you. That's some Crip shit foreal, so I sent the video out to the Damu homies. See if they know who these clown niggas are."

Caesar shook his head. "Good thinking. When we find out who they are, they're dead men. Fuck the jewelry. They violated me and my lady. They gotta go," he said and knocked his drink back, getting ready to make another.

Los could tell this was bothering him. "Yeah don't trip. I got you. We'll know who they are by the end of the night. My word."

Caesar looked at him and said, "You're proving to be invaluable, lil brother. Take care of this within 48 hours, I'll drop my price on the pack to an even ticket."

Boogie looked at Los and couldn't believe their good luck. The Game Gods had truly been blessing them lately.

He spoke up. “My brother’s word is bond. Mine is too. These niggas won’t be breathing before the weekend is over.”

“Straight up,” Los said, agreeing with him.

“Remember what I said about everything in-house, that way the money always stays home? This is a prime example, killers on deck. No need to contact an outsider for a job we can do and have him be a liability. Plus I rather see you ball, my young friends,” Caesar said to both of them.

Chapter 27

"This Brazo right here," Los said to Boogie as they were driving off Caesar's property. He answered it on Bluetooth.

"My boy. You on speaker. Boogie in the car with me," Los said.

"What's bracking with my brothers?" Brazo said over the car speakers.

"You get the video I sent you? Who is them niggas with the Baby A's?" Los asked him.

"Yeah. I asked a few of the homies and that's Stink Locc and G from Charity Homes Crip out in Phoenix. We funk with them niggas heavy," Brazo answered.

"Yeah we on they ass too. Where they be at?" Los said, praying his homie knew the answer.

"They got a trap in them blue apartments on 44th out in North Phoenix. Stink got a black Crown Vic on rims," Brazo told him, making Los' job easier.

"Good look, my nigga. I'ma hit you tomorrow," Los said and hung up.

He looked over at Boogie and said, "How you tryna do it?"

"If we hit they trap, then definitely gotta bring the team out. If we wait and try and catch him at his load it can be me and you. I'm with whatever," Boogie said, loading a 100-round double nutz clip into his own Baby AR-15.

"Let's slide out to Phoenix and see what it's looking like," Los said and hopped on I-10 going north.

***

"This they trap? This why that nigga drive a Crown Vic in 2022?" Boogie said, referring to the dead quiet, empty apartment complex.

"Yeah this aint bracking at all. It's almost 5 a.m. and no smokers out. Dry as fuck," Los commented.

"I don't see no Crown Vic either. Let's drive around and look for them niggas," Boogie said, getting restless.

"Say less, ma boy. Say less," Los told him, pulling out of the parking lot.

They drove around for 30 minutes and found themselves in an industrial area by Old Indian School Road. Boogie seen that the strip club they just passed was still open.

"Pull up into that parking lot, brother," he told Los.

Los hit a U-turn and pulled into the parking lot of The Vault strip club, the old V-Live. After seeing there were no spaces, he pulled onto the street to try and find a spot out there. "Aint that a bitch. Look at what we have here," he said to Boogie, staring at a black Crown Vic on rims.

"Park and let's go inside. See if these niggas up in there," Boogie said excitedly.

"Damn nigga. You sound excited. Let me find out you a serial killer now, brother," Los joked.

They parked the car and went into the strip club. The bouncer was wanding niggas so they had to leave the poles in the car.

They got in and almost instantly caught a contact high. The way the lights in the club was, you could see clouds of blue blunt smoke in the air. They got to the bar and ordered a couple shots.

Los got his drink and put his back to the bar. "You see these niggas up in here?" he asked Boogie, looking for them in the club.

"Shit, they came up tonight. They probably in the back blowing the bag on some pussy that a nigga like me get for free," Boogie said.

"Out of all the shit them niggas could've done with' that bag, you probably right," Los said, agreeing with him and shaking his head at the trick nigga tendencies. "That's why they trap look like that. Them niggas blowing the re-up on some pussy."

***

"Yeah bitch. Just like that," Stink Locc said to the stripper giving him head in the private room. He had a stack of ones, dropping them onto her sweaty body while she performed oral sex.

He was feeling like a million bucks. He had on Caeser's diamond Cuban link chain and a pocket full of blue faces. He was finna drop 8k tomorrow on a used Benz. His lil homie G Locc was in the next room paying a stripper for some pussy too.

Their plug wasn't fucking with them anymore so their trap was dry. They needed this lick tonight to survive. After he copped the Benz, he was finna grab a 9-pack of soft from his cousin with the rest of Caeser's money and bubble back up. They didn't know death was literally around the corner.

"Aagghhh," he said while shooting his load down her throat. He dropped the rest of the ones on the floor for her then zipped up and got up outta there.

He knocked on G's door and said, "I'ma be at the bar waiting for you. Hurry that ass up." He heard the stripper in there moaning. He jiggled the door knob a few times, laughed, and went to the bar.

He pulled out a blue hunnid and told the bartender, "Get me a double shot of that XO Remy. Two of 'em. And keep the change."

"Money go fast when you aint earn it," the man standing at the bar next to him said

"Excuse me, muthafucka. Do I know you, cuzz? Thought so. Mind ya business," he said back, then unconsciously touched the Cuban.

The man next to him finished his drink and left.

The interaction had the already drunk Stink Locc feeling tougher than he was.

Always a nigga around that got something to say, hating. Talking 'bout my money... nigga, where yours at? he said to himself as he knocked back the first double shot.

G finally came from the private room area in the back of the club.

"Enjoy yo self, lil homie? That bitch sound like she was crawling up the wall!" Stink said, and they both started laughing.

***

"Here them niggas come right now," Los whispered to Boogie as they stood in the shadows, waiting on their prey to get closer. "I want the Stink nigga. The one in the white tee. Matter fact, sit back and learn how to really kill a nigga. Cover me if shit get too tricky."

"Blood, why you tryna get fancy? Let's kill these niggas and go," Boogie said.

"Bloody, just cover me like I said."

Los half-walked, half-stumbled up to the two men with one hand behind his back, the other in front of him with a cigarette, pretending to be sloppy drunk.

"One of y'all got a lighter?" he said, purposely slurring his words.

He caught them off guard and fell into Stink and shot him twice in the stomach with a silenced Ghost Glock Boogie had brought from Portland.

PFFT! PFFT!

G didn't recognize the sounds his ears were hearing so he was clueless that Stink had just been shot. Los pulled back from Stink and fired into G's face.

PFFT! PFFT! PFFT!

He ran through their pockets and snatched the chain off Stink's neck and noticed he was still alive. "King Caeser sent me. Bitch ass nigga."

Stink remembered the name and panicked, putting his hands up to block the shots and said, "He... he... he can have the money and jewelry back. P-p-please don't kill me."

"Bitch ass nigga. Shut the fuck up," Los growled and fired into his face.

PFFT! PFFT! PFFT!

"Come on, extra ass nigga," Boogie said to him, pulling on his arm to go.

Los looked at him and smiled. "I'm artistic with' this shit, brother."

They ran back to the car and sped off into the night, happy to put in work for Caeser.

Chapter 28

Melody received the invite to her daughter Kaleah's wedding in the desert two weeks before it was scheduled to take place. She looked at the email and was happy her daughter had found love and planned to make the trip out to Arizona with her sister that week to help them with the planning of the wedding.

***

"Jefe, I got some good news for you this morning," Juan told Bird over the phone. "I've been monitoring Kaleah Bay's mother's email and this morning she got a wedding invitation. We know the time, place, and date when her and Los tie the knot."

This was definitely good news. Bird was down on the scoreboard and was in desperate need of some points.

"Send the details to Maria. And tell her to come see me in the main house for lunch today. Good job, mijo," Bird said and hung up.

He couldn't wait for Los to be out of the picture. Since the night Eddy was murdered, it had been quiet on both sides. Bird preferred it that way though.

Let them think I've taken my L's and went home, he thought. *They had another thing coming.* Los owed Bird some family members. This blood debt was about to be paid in full.

"Ahhh. My beautiful Maria. How's the training going?" Bird asked her when she sat down at the table for lunch with him.

"It's going great. Mario says I'm the best weapon in your arsenal and I agree with him. If I can be honest with you though, Jefe? I'm tired of just training. I want to get in the field and put this training to use..." she told him.

Bird observed his female killing machine with proud, loving eyes. Like a parent views their child taking their first steps.

"Well then I've got some great news for you, hermana. You received Juan's email, sí? Then you know about Los' upcoming wedding..." He said that last part and observed her closely to see if she had any emotional reaction to what he was telling her. "I want you and Mario in Arizona by tomorrow. Crash that wedding. I don't want one of them to make it to the altar. You can choose which one."

Maria's heart was thumping in her chest. This was the reason she woke up every day and trained for hours in the hot, dry Sinaloan desert. It was all for this. She wouldn't disappoint.

"Gracias, brother. I won't let you down. And when I've accomplished what all these men have not, I want my own section of La Familia to run."

"Handle this and I'll see that you have all that and more," Bird said as he put the fork to a piece of shrimp and ate it.

"Then I'll leave you to your meal. I've got preparations to make," Maria said and left the dining room.

Maria, Mario, and Juan arrived in Phoenix the next day. Since Sinaloa was so close to Arizona, they were smuggled over the border with all the weapons they would need for the job. They were staying at a property owned by a La Familia shell corporation put together by Juan. He came to help with the surveillance. He was gifted in all things electrical and technical.

Their plan was to stake out the church the wedding was at and follow Kaleah home. They were undecided about kidnapping her. Even though Los had chosen her over Maria, Maria had known about Kaleah since day one and chosen to accept it. Her beef wasn't with her. Plus, she was a woman, and Maria wasn't about to let Mario or Juan get their hands on her. If any of them took out Kaleah, it was going to be her. This was her mission. They were just here to provide support.

***

Juan sat in the back of the white panel van a half block down from the church. The van's exterior was equipped with audio and visual enhancements. He had his meth pipe out and was blowing clouds in nerd, tweaker heaven.

This was his first time in the field and he was under major pressure to perform correctly. He wasn't sure he would survive any fuck-ups. When this was over and they were all back in Mexico, he was gonna ask Bird to be trained in guns and combat like Maria was. He loved this spy shit. So far nothing interesting had happened. Kaleah arrived with two women he didn't recognize, but both he would fuck. He would run their faces through his recognition software when he got back to the house.

He wondered if Maria might let him fuck while they were on this trip. She surely wasn't fucking the anti-social Mario or the sadistic cartel leader that Bird was. When he was high, anything was possible.

He finished programming the GPS magnet to activate only while the car was driving, to save battery life. Now would be the hard part: get close enough to their vehicle to plant it.He looked at the cameras and made sure nobody was looking, then got out of the back of the van carrying a clipboard as a decoy and hurried up the street. He got to the church parking lot and approached the matte pink Benz truck and looked around, head on a swivel. Confident the coast was clear, he dropped down and stuck the magnet under the front bumper. He tied his shoe, got up, and hurried back to the vehicle.

Seconds later he was back inside the safety of the surveillance van and his heart was thumping in his chest. Hard. He was glad he was alone—the others would see the unfamiliarity of this whole thing broadcasted on his face. At least he managed to plant the bug without being seen. Now with that done, he could return to the house. His task done for the day.

***

"Girl, some Mexican kid was just acting strange around your car," Kayla told Liv after observing Juan from a church window, unseen.

"Strange? Strange like how? Don't play with' me, Kayla," Liv told her.

"No, I'm foreal. It might be nothing. It probably is. I just seen him duck next to it then get up and hurry off. It's still there though, I guess that's all that matters," Kayla reassured her.

"Duck next to it? He was probably tying his shoe, girl. Don't get my blood pressure going for nothing like that again. Foreal," Liv said with an attitude.

Even though Kaleah had chosen to give her a pass and accept her into their sisterhood, Liv was still unsure about her.

"You guys ready to go?" Kaleah said, walking up, done with the decorators for the day.

***

They pulled up to the mini mansion and Los and Boogie were out front washing their cars. Liv parked behind Los' matte grey Hellcat Durango, hopped out, and said, "Brother, you got mine when you done?" in her sweetest voice possible.

He looked at her and shook his head, "I got you, sis," and went to help Kaleah out of the car.

"Look at you. Acting like you love me," she joked. They kissed and she went inside to escape the heat.

Los finished the Durango and started on Liv's Benz truck. He was hitting it with the hose when something fell from underneath the bumper.

"What in the fuck is this?" he said after picking it up.

He showed it to Boogie.

"That's a GPS magnet, brother," he said, confirming Los' suspicion.

He went inside and found Liv sitting in the kitchen.

"Sis, what the fuck is this?" he asked her. "You see who put this on yo shit? This fell off yo truck."

"Noooo, brother. Kayla told me she saw a Mexican boy acting strange around my car, but that was it. He must've put it there," she told him.

Los went upstairs to Kayla's room. The door was open. "Kay, you seen who put this on Liv's truck today?" he asked her.

"So that's what the fuck he was doing," she said, shaking her head. "Yeah bro. It was a Mexican boy. Like a teenager or small man in his 20s. Skinny. Short."

Her FBI training kicked in and she started describing him.

"A Mexican, huh? I was wondering when they would show up around here. Good eyes though. Just hypothetically, what do you think should be done in this situation?" he asked her, picking her brain.

"If I was you and didn't want them knowing that I knew they were tracking you and that this was the destination, I'd take that GPS and put it back underneath her bumper and take her car somewhere else. This is our home. And even though we're capable of defending it, we still shouldn't compromise it. You feel me?" she said.

"I love it. Took the thoughts right out of my brain! See, this is why I kept you around, sis! It's always good to have an educated, strategic thinker available," Los told her. "I'm a go handle this business. Keep a pole close to you at all times and stay by LeeLee in case they already coming. I'll be back soon."

It went without saying that when Los wasn't around, it was Kayla's responsibility to keep LeeLee alive.

He walked back outside and hopped in Liv's truck. He told Boogie to follow him. He drove the truck to the house the homies were renting a few miles away from their own and parked it down the block. After that, he went inside to give them instructions.

"Someone placed a GPS unit on Liv's truck today. Kayla said it was a Mexican boy. There's no shortage of them around, but assume he's with La Familia. She drove it to the crib without knowing. It fell off when she parked in the driveway. I found it by accident. I put it back under the bumper and drove that muthafucka up the street from here. Keep an eye on it. Anything suspicious, shoot first, deal with the fallout later. Understood?" he asked the room.

"So let me get this straight," Juice said from the couch, pausing his 2k game. "Instead of them knowing where y'all live, you brought that muthafucka over here? You not shit." He finished and shook his head.

"Bitch, it aint in y'all driveway, so stop crying. Y'all niggas knew we was gon' have to deal with these niggas again sooner or later. Just keep your eyes open and a pole next to you, brother. That's all I'm saying," Los told him.

"Yeah, yeah. You good, brother. Shit been too quiet anyway. You and Boog been having all the action lately. It's our turn," Kapone said and racked the lever on his full-sized AR-10 with Cinnabon underneath.

He had just got back in town from Vegas that day. Since he wasn't in Portland the day the trooper got smoked and wasn't with Los and Boog at the warehouse that night, he was good. He had no warrants and was still able to wiggle from state to state without looking over his shoulder. He used a whole different identity whenever he flew into Arizona though. The FBI knew he was Mafia, and he wasn't about to lead them to his niggas inadvertently.

"Ma nigga," Boogie said, laughing, then shook his hand.

"Hit my line if anything look tricky. I'm a be here in the morning to take it back to the church," Los said, then him and Boogie left.

"Tomorrow we gon' drive it back to the church and act like everything is normal. After that we gon' park up the street and see if they come back. I don't like this shit, Boog," Los told him, sitting in the passenger seat of Boogie's EXT Escalade, going back home.

"Me neither, bro. But you seem like you got it figured out. So now aint nothing to it but to do it. On a separate note. Them packs Caesar had dropped off? I took 'em to HP and he cooked a few, he said they so raw he turning 1 into 2! Them smokers going Krazy off these new joints!" he said, excitedly.

"Hell the fuck yeah. You finna have yo own mansion soon, brother. Shit, grab that muthafucka across the street from us. Lil Tony can get you a deal on that shit right now. You know what I'm a do with my first few millions, brother? I'm a buy every house on the block next to me. Control the neighborhood. Leave a few empty for family and rent the rest out to muthafuckas that would never get a chance to live in something luxurious like that. You feel me?" Los told him.

Boogie nodded his head. "Sound like a plan to me, brother. I respect it."

"Ownership. After that block, then buy the next one and so on and so on. 'til the whole neighborhood is Black and Brown. Lee and Liv got that salon. I'm a slide baby a smooth million and tell her to franchise them joints in Phoenix, Scottsdale, and Tucson. I'm a grind this shit out with my niggas for the next few years, then y'all can have that shit. Hopefully by that time we all owners," Los said, optimistically.

"I see yo vision, bro, and been thinking 'bout what I'm a do with my money lately too. Kayla is pregnant and I got my 2 back in the town. I'm tryna leave a legacy for my seeds."

"No more Chevy vans?" Los said, and they laughed. "That's what's important though, bro. And that's what we doing it for. I can't wait for bro to come home so he can ball with us. Caesar said by the end of the year. But you know how that shit go. Long as my nigga coming home sooner than later, we good."

***

While Maria and Mario drove to where the GPS said the truck was located to do some reconnaissance, Juan was at the house putting together dossiers of each known Mafia member. He had ran the 2 women with Kaleah last through his facial recognition software and came up with one being her sister. The other was a dead end. She literally didn't exist. This just sparked his interest even more, and he decided to hack into a few databases to see what he could dig up.

He logged into the backdoor he had set up into the FBI's system and ran her face through there.

"Kayla Lopez, huh?" Juan said out loud to himself.

Surprisingly, her file was blank after that. Which was odd. He double-backed into the CIA database, and it had little more information to offer. College on the East Coast, Ivy League, graduated top of her class, then nothing after that...

What the fuck!

He wasn't used to not being able to accomplish something he set out to do while on his supercomputer.

This bitch is either a spy or never broke a law in her life!

After an hour of digging, he gave up and lit up his pipe. After blowing a few clouds, he decided he was done for the night. He checked in with Maria and asked how her night was going. She was short with him and hung up.

Must be that time of the month, he thought. *There goes my chances of a quick fuck. But her mouth isn't bleeding...*

The meth had his mind moving a mile a minute and he decided he wouldn't press his luck this trip...

There's always next time!

***

After driving by a few times, Maria and Mario decided to walk by and check out the house on foot. Check for weak spots and plan a strategy in case they had to go inside. They had decided if any of the people living there were outside slipping, they would give them a pass. No need to blow up the spot on a non-factor when Los was almost certainly nearby. For now, they had the advantage of being an unknown hostile. They wanted to remain inconspicuous for the time being.

They walked past the pink Benz and looked at the house it was parked in front of. The curtains in a front window were parted, and the window was open, letting in that cool desert night breeze, and they could see inside. What they saw wasn't what they thought they would be seeing? What was an older white woman doing sitting on the couch with a cat next to her? Where the fuck was Los? Or Kaleah? Or her fucking sister? Did they know Juan planted a tracker on her car? Maybe this was the wrong house. All these thoughts ran through Maria's mind when she looked into that window.

***

Juice and Kapone had been watching the street traffic on and off ever since Los had stopped by and told them to be on point. So far, it was the same usual cars and people that occupied the neighborhood.

Kapone was taking the trash to the curb for pickup the next morning when he noticed a Mexican couple staring into the window of the house down the block. Now this definitely wasn't usual. He hurried into the house and told Juice to strap up, it might get tricky.

Kapone went to the upstairs bedroom facing the street and hid in the shadows of the window. He took out his iPhone and started to film the couple looking into the window of the next house and arguing, getting both their faces and them speed walking away to a black Tahoe. He sent the video to Los immediately.

***

DING!

Los picked up his phone right away and saw Kapone had sent him a video with the words *"watch rn!"* under it. He clicked on the video and pressed play. What he saw blew his mind!

Was that Maria? In Arizona? It couldn't be! But deep down he knew it was her after slowing the video down and pressing pause on her face shot. Now his next thoughts were, *What the fuck was she doing with the muthafucka from the warehouse?* He laughed at the ridiculousness of this shit. *This bitch couldn't come with me so now she against me... But how the fuck she get involved with Bird and them?*

He decided to give her a ring and act like he was checking up on her. Surprisingly, she picked up after the first two rings. *This gon' always be my bitch*, he thought and smirked to himself.

"Mamacita! How you been, baby?" he asked after she said hello.

"Los... finally decided to do the right thing and check up on me... months later," she told him.

"Shit been hectic. You know how it be... I never stopped thinking 'bout you though. I told you shit was 'bout to get tricky so get out the way. You still at your grandma's?"

"Am I still at my grandmother's... actually no. I'm not. I'm here and there. Doing me. I'm actually living my best life... if you cared to know. Anything new in your life?" she asked him, hoping he would at least keep it real about getting fucking married! But that was too much to ask.

"Living yo best life huh? I love that for you, foreal. You always gon' be my day one. I had to shake the town though. Shit got hot like I told you it would. I'm in Arizona now doing my thing. Hit me if you ever out this way... You know you my day one and we always gon' share that. No matter who come in our life, we was there first. Remember that when them nerd niggas get to polluting your mind 'bout a nigga and our bond. It's nobody business but our business," he told her, getting deep. *Trying to mind fuck her into not doing something Krazy! The audacity of this bitch to fuck with my opps!*

Maria was quiet for a second while she soaked in his words. She could feel old feelings tugging at her heartstrings. She had to remember her training and stick to the mission. *But could she really?*

"Well, Los, I love that for you too. And I'll keep that in mind if I'm ever in Arizona. Hitting you will definitely be on the to-do list for sure. Gotta go. Take care," she said and hung up before he had her compromising the mission before it truly started.

***

"Don't say a fucking word to me about whatever you think you just heard," Maria said to Mario while they drove back to the house.

"You mean you reminiscing with your boyfriend? You sure you can put whatever the fuck you're obviously feeling right now behind you and complete what we came out here to do?" Mario asked her. He had orders to kill her if she froze up and couldn't get it done. Life was tricky in the cartel business!

"What you heard was me getting closure on a big chapter of my life. What do you think I meant when I said *'hitting him will definitely be on the to-do list whenever I was in Arizona'*? What the fuck do you think *'hitting him will definitely be on the to-do list'* meant? You know what? Fuck off! And mind your own business!" she said that last part with major attitude and gave him that look that said *I can kill you with my bare hands*. She turned the radio on and turned it up. *Fuck both of you*, she thought to herself, pissed off at being questioned. *Or was she mad that Los had her feeling some type of way?*

Chapter 29

A few hours later, Juan was high, playing *World of Warcraft* on his computer, and Mario was asleep. Maria was awake in her room going over the dossiers that Juan had prepared for them. She was taught to *Know Thy Enemy.* And would definitely not underestimate Los or his team.

She got to Los' file and paused before reading it. She was overwhelmed with the feelings of guilt and betrayal. And the picture of him attached to the file had them heartstrings tugging again!

Maria closed her eyes and laid her head back on the pillow and relaxed on the Tempur-Pedic king-size bed. The ripping and running she'd done since getting back in the States had her more tired than she thought—she was exhausted, actually. Soon she was in a deep sleep...

"Mamacita! Give Papi some sugar!" Los said and swept her off her feet into a bear hug, kissing her neck then lips. He asked her, "Who you love?"

"You, Papi! Always you!" she told him, then bit his bottom lip when he kissed her.

Maria's young ass was in love! Them boys she dated back in high school could never compare to her Los! And she just knew he felt the same way.

"Baby, them other bitches is strictly paying me. Word up. You think all this shit around you free? Nah. This shit cost! But fuck them bitches—let's me and you get some money and shit on them hoes together," Los said to the 18-year-old Maria, looking into her eyes while he said this.

"I'm down to ball with you, baby... but my job only pays so much," Maria said, referring to her part-time gig at her aunt's taqueria.

"Nah, baby. Fuck that job. I know the way, go the way, and for the right girl I show the way. Baby, do you trust me?" he asked her, still looking at her with his captivating green eyes.

"I trust you so much, Papi..." she said, in love with him more than anything in this moment.

"Then trust I'll never lead you the wrong way, and trust I'd never judge you for anything you do for us. I need you to leave all that high school, kid shit behind you and step into a grown woman's lane, and let me make you a bad boss bitch foreal, standing next to yo boss ass nigga... You down for me like I'm down for you, Mami?"

"I wanna step into a grown woman's lane and be your queen, my king. I'll do anything for you, Los. I'm down foreal," she told him. And that had been her start into the game. Before she knew it, she was in the club seven nights a week with a $500 quota every night. Los wanted $10k every 20 days, and she was down to get it for them.

But she soon learned it gets grimy behind the scenes of all that stunting. She had seen Los sniff cocaine before—when they were on the road going to a club OT, he would often hit the sack while driving to stay up. Or so he claimed. So she wasn't a stranger to drugs; she just had never done them personally. That soon changed.

Los had been giving her an 8-ball of powder every night to take to work with her and sell it to the strippers.

"Amina! Your man has the best shit I've ever had! Do some with me!" her stripper friend had told her in the dressing room at work. If it was alright for her nigga to do it, then it was alright for her. That first time turned into every time... She soon found herself with a habit.

She tried to hide the severity of it from Los. But him being a cocaine user himself, he knew the signs. The first thing he noticed was her sudden, rapid weight loss. She went from slim thick to just slim. She would often get home from work still high and barely get any sleep. But the makeup could only hide the bags underneath her eyes for so long.

And that was the first time Los had lied to her. His first betrayal. He did judge her. She was fucking up the money getting high, and he wasn't happy. All of a sudden she was a "dope head bitch," whenever he was mad at her. Never once apologizing for how he was treating her.

He eventually started fucking with other bitches and not giving her his full attention like he used to. He was breaking her heart every day and didn't care. But she still loved him deep in her soul.

This motivated her to get clean and stop using. But even after she was sober and back on track, things were never the same. He would just string her along, giving her just enough attention to keep her around. He didn't wanna be with her, but he for damn sure didn't want her with nobody else. And it had been like that ever since...

Maria woke out of her sleep suddenly, but thankful she was no longer in that dream down memory lane! Everybody has different definitions for nightmares, and to her, that was one indeed. *She didn't need that right now when she had a mission to complete!*

Oh Los... why'd you have to do me like this again and again... Maria thought, thinking about how her dream was still her reality. *If I can't have you... nobody can...* was her last thought before falling back into a dreamless sleep.

"Jefe... I'm losing confidence in Maria... She was on the phone with Los last night going down memory lane. She's been in her room ever since we got back last night," Mario told Bird. "You know what to do if she freezes up. That's why I sent both of you. I'll call her today and check her temperature también. For now, continue with plan A. The wedding is still a week away. I know they have a trap out there somewhere, and I want you to find it and shut it down.

I have soldiers coming to meet you later today. You're in charge, Mario. Don't fail me. Where's Juan?" Bird asked. "He's here. That boy doesn't sleep."

"I don't pay him to sleep. Keep him busy. I gotta go," Bird said and hung up.

Keep him busy? Mario thought. *Looks like Juan is jumping off the porch today!*

"Juan!" Mario shouted. "¡Ven aquí!"

Juan walked into the room. "¿Qué pasó, hermano?"

"Put your shoes on. You're outside with me today!" Mario said and laughed.

***

"Pull up to the church. Let's check that out first," Mario told Juan, riding shotgun in the panel van.

Juan did as he was told and drove by the church, seeing the matte pink Benz truck like yesterday. He double backed and parked down the block.

***

"These muthafuckas was dumb enough to come back the next day," Boogie said, shaking his head and laughing at the stupidity. "What you tryna do?" he asked Los.

Los called Kapone and told him to put it on speaker. "That white van that just pulled up in front of you? That's them. Start yo car. When I drive by, get behind me. We finna bounce out on these muthafuckas," Los said.

"Say less," Kapone said, while Juice slapped the Cinnabon underneath the AR-10.

Half a minute later, Los drove by them in the Durango. They pulled out behind him. Los slammed the brakes, and Boogie was out the door before he had it in park.

"Bitch ass niggas! Put yo hands up!" he screamed at Juan and Mario.

Fuck! Mario swore under his breath, recognizing Los walking around the truck. He looked to his right and Juice was there with the AR-10 pointed at him. He could smell the urine running down Juan's pants leg.

"Get the fuck out this car!" Los said, opening the door of the van and snatching Mario out, while Boogie pulled out Juan.

"So we meet again," Los said, then pistol-whipped him, knocking him out.

"Help me get this nigga into the back of the van. Then zip tie him," he said to Juice. "You heard that, Boog?"

Twenty seconds later, Juan and Mario were in the back of the panel van, zip tied and knocked out.

"Boog, get behind the wheel. I'm finna tell Lee Lee to take the Durango home."

***

Thirty minutes later, Juan and Mario were both tied to chairs in the basement of the Casa Grande trap house, still unconscious. Los ran through Mario's pockets and pulled out Mario's burner phone. He went to the call log and called the last dialed number. He recognized Bird's voice as the one that answered.

"My friend. We aint spoke in a while..." Los told him.

"Carlos... You keep proving yourself to be a worthy adversary. I assume you have my man tied up somewhere in a dark place."

"Then you assume correctly. All this could've been avoided, you know? Yo rat ass brother tried to get over on me for 5 boats. Thought shit was sweet. So I broke his nose. Then I killed him a few weeks later. Your brother was a worm that thought he was a snake just 'cuz he slithered. But he had no real power. I hit you to make that shit right and you ignored me. Then y'all popped my bitch. Shit been up ever since. Now I'm coming for you, Bird. Hope you left a spot open next to yo brother and niece."

Bird was shocked at what he was hearing. It made sense though. This wasn't the first time he heard about Eddy getting over on his clients. But too much blood had been shed to make this right though. He would lose respect. And respect was what kept you alive in this business.

"This is my first time hearing about this situation with you and Eduardo. I always wondered what made you strike out against me, little brother. Of course you know this revelation changes nothing. My mother shed tears 'cause of you. My niece, Los? Really? Go ahead and kill Mario! I have a thousand Marios to replace him!" Bird screamed into the phone and hung up.

Los set the burner phone on the ground and smashed it with a hammer.

"Wake these bitch ass niggas up!" he told Boogie.

Boogie threw a cup of cold water in both of their faces. "Wakey wakey," he said and laughed.

Mario opened his eyes and seen a group of demons. Los had HP shut the trap down while he conducted this interrogation. The whole team was there. He looked to the side and seen Juan with duct tape over his mouth, eyes wide with fear and panic.

"My boss is going to kill each of you slowly," Mario threatened.

"Oh yeah? That same boss that just told me to go ahead and kill you?" Los asked him.

HP tapped Kapone and whispered, "This yo first interrogation with bro? He 'bout to go krazy." He said it loud enough for Mario and Juan to hear.

"HP? Grab me that nail gun. Niggas wanna be tough. Let's see how tough they is," Los said, grabbing the nail gun from HP.

"Boog? Remember we gave this bitch a pass at the warehouse? You was right, we should've killed everyone there. Well, we learn from our mistakes over here. Put that tape back on his mouth."

Boogie put a rag in Mario's mouth and taped it closed. Then Los shot him in both kneecaps with the nail gun. Mario was screaming and thrashing in the seat. Juan was next to him watching this go down, sweating bullets.

"Anybody want some of this action?" Los asked the room.

"Shiiit, let me see that muthafucka!" Juice said excitedly, taking the nail gun from Los and shooting Mario in the legs, stomach, and chest.

"What about this nigga?" Juice said, referring to Juan.

"Nah. I gotta feeling he's gonna be more cooperative than this one," Los said, then looked at Kapone and told him, "Smoke this nigga, blood."

"My pleasure!" Kapone said, hitting the switch on his Glock 23 and squeezing the trigger. Shooting Mario in the face 20 times.

Los squatted in front of Juan and tore the tape off his mouth. Juan instantly started stuttering.

"I-I-I'll tell you whatever you want. P-p-please don't kill me," he pleaded.

"Did you plant a tracker on a pink truck yesterday?" Los asked him.

"Yes, I did. Look, I just d-d-do the computer shit. I don't kill anybody!"

"Calm down. Tell the truth and you might survive this day. How many people does Bird have with y'all on this mission?"

"Just me, Maria, and him," he said, nudging his elbow in Mario's direction.

"Maria? What's her role in all this?"

"This is her mission. I just do surveillance. No offense, man, but Maria hates you. Mario was just here in case she got cold feet and couldn't pull the trigger," Juan said, hoping the truth would set him free.

Los laughed at Juan's answer. "Maria's mission? Now I know you lying! Maria wouldn't hurt a fly! She's not no killer!"

"Maria's been in Mexico with us the last few months, training every day for this. She does hand-to-hand combat with Tito fucking Ortiz and shoots on the range every day. She's very committed."

"I bet. What do y'all know about my family up here?"

"Nothing. Believe me. We just got here 2 days ago. I planted the GPS and that's it. Last night they went by where the truck was parked but didn't see you guys. That's it. I swear," Juan said, starting to cry.

"What's the plan? When is she supposed to kill me? And what's the address to y'all safehouse?""1602 Natasha Way. Casa Grande. That's where we're staying. The plan is for either you or your fiancée to not make it to the altar. Bird doesn't care which one..."

At the mention of his fiancée, Los backhanded Juan, knocking 2 of his teeth out. "That's how Bird wants to play this shit huh? Bet!" Los said, heading for the stairs. "Knock this nigga back out and take him back to the van. Wrap the dead nigga up in that sheet and take him up there too. I gotta call to make."

Los went upstairs and called Kayla. "Stay close to Lee Lee. Don't let her out of your sight. We caught the Mexicans out by the church and we're interrogating them right now. The house is safe. But the wedding has to change locations. Keeping Kaleah alive is all that matters though. You got it?" he asked.

"I got you, bro. Lee Lee is my sister. Don't worry about it," Kayla told him.

"Say less..." Los told her and hung up. He walked into the garage and seen them loading the bodies back into the panel van.

"Kapone, follow them niggas back to the church and bring 'em back here when they drop the van back off. We finna slide by they safehouse."

"I got you, brother," Kapone said, still pumped up from killing Mario.

***

"Mari, Los has Mario and Juan. Assume they're not coming back. Take what you need and leave there immediately. The mission is still on. I'm sending you more soldiers tonight," Bird told Maria.

"¡Pinche pendejos! How the fuck did they get caught slipping? I got you, Jefe. I'm packing my shit up right now! Send me the address!" Maria said and hung up the phone.

She was in a rush to get out of there ASAP! She knew Juan or Mario probably gave this address up and Los probably had his team on the way right now! She never unpacked all the way, so all she did was throw her bags in the truck with an armful of clothes, then went back inside for the guns and was gone from the house within 5 minutes of the phone call.

Fucking amateurs! she thought about Juan and Mario. *Why the fuck would he take Juan into the field with him? Risking our best tech guy for nothing! Oh well! Now I can be Mano De Jefe!* were her thoughts as she drove off the property of the compromised safehouse.

***

Juan had to breathe through his nose as he lay under Mario's corpse in the back of the panel van. Mario had shit himself when he died and that's all Juan smelled.

Fuck the odor! I'm just happy to be alive! he thought. He had definitely dodged a bullet! Literally!

He had to warn Maria that they were coming for her! And let Bird know. He wasn't afraid of Bird killing him for this. This was Mario's fault. Plus, he was too valuable to the operation as a whole to be killed for another's mistake.

He felt the car slowing down, then felt it stop all the way. He closed his eyes and prayed they wouldn't decide to kill him next! He heard the doors open and shut. Then he heard them drive off.

He decided to stay in the back under the corpse for a few more minutes just in case they came back. After what seemed like forever, he crawled from underneath Mario and opened the back doors. He got out and threw up instantly. He got back into the van and closed the doors. He got on his computer and called Bird.

"Jefe! I'm alive!" he said when Bird answered.

"What about Mario? Where are you?"

"Mario is dead! They dropped me back off at the church! I don't know where to go! Before Mario died, he told them about the safehouse!" he lied.

"Maria is already in the wind. Don't go there. Here's the address. Head there immediately," Bird told him and hung up. Happy that his best hacker was still alive, Los had took too much from him already.

Chapter 30

"Do you, Kaleah Bay, take Carlos Mills—" the priest was saying when he was interrupted by a loud boom as the doors to the church were kicked in. Maria rushed in with Mack at her side, followed by soldiers, and started shooting up the wedding.

Kayla rushed the altar, grabbing Kaleah's hand and pulling her to the back of the church for safety. Los pulled out his gold-plated Glock 20 and started shooting everything moving. From the corner of his eye, he saw Boogie go down with a shot to the head.

"Boogie!" he yelled and smoked the soldier that killed Boogie. He saw Maria in the chaos in that moment, shooting the people that came to the wedding and laughing as she did it. Mack was next to her, shooting into the crowd also.

Los was surrounded. For every one that he killed, two more popped up. He slapped in a new clip and kept getting busy! He felt a hand on his shoulder, and he turned around. At that moment, he felt another one on him, wrestling the gun away from him. The soldiers had him pinned down. Maria and Juice walked up together. They looked at him, helpless, and laughed!

"Ooooh, my poor baby!" Maria said. "If I can't have you, nobody can! I brought your brother that you killed with me to do the job I would feel guilty about later. Don't you feel guilty? Well, I'm gonna let him do the honors while I go grab your bitch! Mack! Kill him for Mami!" she told him, then kissed him on the cheek.

"My pleasure, love," Mack told her.

"You always was a sucka for a bitch!" Los spat at him.

Mack laughed. "See you in hell, brother!"

BOOM! BOOM! BOOM! BOOM!

Los sat up in the bed, rubbing his hands across his chest, feeling the shots he just took in his dream. Thankfully, this nightmare hadn't woken LeeLee up.

She wasn't feeling that they had to change the venue for the wedding, but understood it was for everyone's safety.

Los got up from the bed and went down to the basement. He lit a backwood that was sitting in the ashtray and smoked. This was the first nightmare that he had since leaving Portland. Arizona represented peace to him. He blew clouds of the Gelato and laughed at the irony of this shit! In order to obtain the peace he wanted, he had to embrace the chaos of the past and present. He had to cut the head off the snake. Bird was too dangerous to let live. He decided to call Maria again. She picked up on the second ring.

"Carlos... to what do I owe this pleasure? You calling me two nights in a row hasn't happened since I was a lil girl. What do you want?"

"So you're in town with a mission to kill me, I hear."

"So you believe everything you hear now?" she said to him.

"Cut the shit, Maria! How you gon' link with my opps and make a move against me? Bitch, are you out of your muthafucking mind? You with Bird now and think shit sweet like I won't send my hitters to yo granny house in West Salem, bitch? Like I won't have them niggas burn down yo aunty taco spot with her in it! Bitch, don't fucking play with me!" Los yelled into the phone. "You in way over yo head, Maria. I'ma give you a pass though on the strength of our past and let you live! What did you think you were going to accomplish with killing me or my bitch? How much is he paying you?"

"See Los, the thing is... he's not paying me a dime. What I want can't be bought. After you're gone, I'll have my own cartel. I'll be a boss bitch by myself! Without your help!" she screamed back at him.

"Baby, that's what you want? To be a cartel boss? Fuck with me and let's kill Bird together. That's how you take over. They respect strength. Where you at right now? I'm finna pull up on you... we gon' figure this out tonight." Los said, hoping she would agree.

"Why, Carlos? Why do you want to see me? So you can kill me? Do you think I'm a dumb bitch?" she asked.

"Not at all. If I wanted to kill you, I would come to where the tracker on that van says it's parked at. I'm giving you a chance to redeem yo self with me. Link with me. We can put something together foreal..."

"Well, if you know where I'm at, then come on. No games though, Los. I'm so fucking serious right now." Maria warned.

"Say less... I'm finna be on the way." Los said and hung up.

He called Boogie and woke him up, telling him to come down to the basement. Boogie came down and Los told him his plan to go meet with Maria.

"Bro, are you out of your fucking mind? Did you not hear that lil boy say she been training every day these last few months so she can kill you? This bitch can probably whoop both our ass now! You're tripping," Boogie told him.

"Bro, trust me. This bitch Maria is still my bitch regardless of whatever the fuck she been doing. If we can use her to kill Bird and put her in his spot, then that's two birds with one stone. To be honest, I'm tired of all this looking over my shoulder shit. This isn't what I came out here for. My bitch already got popped for me, now she in danger again? Nah bro. I'm finna nip this in the bud."

"Ma nigga, you help put that bitch in Bird's spot, who's to stop her from coming at us even harder? With all her new resources? Yeah, Bird aint been able to do shit, but who's to say she won't able to get close up on us foreal?"

"She not like that foreal. I don't know what these niggas did to have her switch up on me like this, but I'm finna find out. Follow me bro, and if I don't text you every 30 mins, come in there. The lil boy said it was only them three that came. So I'm assuming it's only her and him in the house. If she don't go for it, then we kill both of them. Word to Slim Ru."

"Aight bro. I'ma rock with you. Let me go put some clothes on and we can dip." Boogie said, reluctantly agreeing with him.

***

Los pulled up to the estate and stopped at the gate. He texted Maria and had her open it. She was standing outside waiting for him.

"We can talk in the car," she said and hopped in the Durango with him. "It's safer this way." She looked at him for a few seconds without saying a word, waiting for him to speak.

"It's nice seeing you..." Los said.

"It's nice seeing me... is that really all you have to say to me, Los? Please don't tell me you woke me up for some bullshit. How about 'my bad for getting engaged on you, Maria'? How about 'I'm sorry for shitting on you after you risked your life for me again? How about starting with that, Los."

"You right. You did risk yo' life with Eddy for me. But we passed that. I was at yo house that night. How many congratulations you want? A fish don't get a pat on the back for swimming. How did they get you to turn against me? I thought we was forever, girl?"

"Apparently, that night I was with Eddy, his man put a tracker on my car. He was into human trafficking. He snatched me up outside my abuelita's house. He was gonna kill me, Los. Then he told me about how you left me to come out here to start a new life. I tried calling you, but you changed your number. What was I to think? I definitely wasn't dying for you at that point. The fuck." Maria said and made a stink face.

"You know why I came out here? I'm on the FBI most wanted list! You see how I changed my face? Shit was hot for me in the town! The night we smoked Eddy, some police got killed too. What was I supposed to do? Stay and go to jail? I was more worried about the police tryna kill me than the suckas! So excuse me for worrying about my life, Maria! I worried about yo ass the night you lined up Eddy though, and what that get me? Some attitude then and you tryna kill me now! So miss me with that extra shit."

"See, I didn't know all that. They got in my head, Los. Took me out to Mexico. I've been Sinaloa training to kill you ever since. My reward for this mission is my own branch of the Cartel. I'll be the boss." Maria said.

"That's what you want? To be the boss?" Los asked her.

"Yeah. But now that we spoke, I don't want you dead. Or hurt. So how can we make that happen? Because I'm not even sure if Bird will let me live if I go back to Mexico empty-handed..."

"I can make that happen for you. Look, I'm tapped in with The Cartel myself. Help me kill Bird and I'll have you put in that top spot. You down?" he said that last part looking into her eyes.

"I'm down, Los. But how are you going to make this happen? What do I do 'til then? I have to at least make some progress out here or he'll think something is up." Maria told him.

"I'll figure something out for you. I'ma hit my nigga and tell him what we tryna do and let you know by the end of tomorrow. Trust me."

"Last time I trusted you I got snatched up outside my grandma's house."

"Man, fuck all that. I got you. Look at me when I talk to you." he said, grabbing her chin and pulling her towards him. "Don't you ever in yo life turn against me again."

She looked at him and said, "Never again... mi corazón es para ti, papi... por siempre..." Then kissed him. "Do we have time to fuck, papi? Please, it's been soooo long!" Maria said, pulling down his sweatpants.

"Yeah, make that shit quick though. What about the lil Mexican boy inside? Where he at?" Los asked while Maria had his dick in her mouth.

"He's asleep. He was up for a week, high. He won't be up for at least 10 more hours. We're good, papi."

"Say less." Los said, then started to fuck her mouth.

Twenty minutes later, Maria was getting out of the truck, high off love. She hoped for her sake that Los would figure something out. Because even though she loved him, she loved herself more. And wouldn't hesitate to take his queen off the chess board to ensure her survival.

"So you want to use this bitch to knock Bird off the top spot?" Caesar asked Los over the phone.

"Yeah. It makes sense. And to have her in his spot would ensure the cooperation of another Organization. This shit with me and Bird is deep. If you choose not to assist me, I'm still killing him..."

"I see," Caesar said, pondering the potential reward and consequences. "I'll be back in town in 2 days. Come to my estate. I'll have an answer for you then."

"Bet. See you then," Los said and hung up.

Regardless of Caesar's help or not, Bird was dying. Now he had to come up with a plan to make sure Maria wasn't going home empty-handed every day.

Chapter 31

"Ma blooda. What's good?" Brazo said, answering the phone.

"Blood. I got a plan for them Charity Homes niggas. Pull up to the trap today," Los told him.

"Say less. Bee you in an hour."

"Whoop," Los said and hung up.

***

Los and Juice sat outside the trap in Los' Durango while Boogie and HP were inside working it. Since Caesar started plugging them, the numbers they were doing had doubled, then tripled! They were waiting on Brazo to show up so Los could tell him his plan.

After 30 more minutes of smoking in the car, popping game, and laughing at the smokers, Brazo pulled up in his red '64 Chevy Impala. He hopped in the back seat of the Durango and pulled out a powder sack. After he hit it a few times, he passed it to the front seat.

"Ma niggas. So what's this plan you talking bout?" he asked them.

Los spoke up after hitting the sack and passing it. "So it aint no secret bout our funk with The Cartel out in Portland. Well, shit been lightweight tricky round here too. I got a plan to have our enemy knock off our enemies," Los said, then told Juice and Brazo about his plan to sic Maria and her goons on the Charity Homes Crip niggas.

"Oowee, that's a muthafucking plan! Remind me to never cross yo conniving ass," Brazo said, and all 3 of them started laughing.

***

"Tamales! Hot tamales! Come and get 'em!" the Tamale Lady yelled as she walked down the block where niggas was hustling. In the middle of the block was an ice cream truck serving the kids.

A Rent-A-Center van was on the block too, so somebody was somewhere getting harassed. Just another busy day in Charity Homes. Quan stood up from the dice game and wiped the sweat off his face—it was hot outside.

"Bitch nigga! Pay me my money!" Luccy yelled at the niggas in the circle and swiped the money off the ground before shaking the dice again. They were in the alley next to the trap house. It was a hot ass day, even for an Arizona summer. So hot the smokers were inside somewhere hiding from the sun.

"That bitch selling them tamales is bad! I'm finna go grab a few! And see what she doing later!" one of the hustlers said.

"I'll tell you what she doing later! Taking that tamale money home to them 5 kids she probably got in that 2-bedroom!" Quan said, causing the group to laugh.

The ice cream truck finished serving the children and was creeping down the block. The Tamale Lady stopped yelling and went up to talk to the ice cream man. A white panel van was coming from the opposite direction.

Quan walked up to the tamale stand and whistled at the lady to come back. She walked up smiling and asked how many he wanted.

He said 2 and turned around to ask if any of his brothers on the block with him wanted any. That was the last thing he did. The Tamale Lady pulled out an MP5 submachine gun from inside the food cart and shot him in the side of the face while he was turned around, knocking chunks off his head.

THRAAATAATATAAT! THRAAATAATATAAT!

As soon as she shot him, shooters poured out of the back of the ice cream truck and the back of the white panel van and started shooting everything moving.

Luccy had turned around when Quan asked if they wanted anything and seen him lose half his face. He didn't freeze up. He drew down instantly and was letting his Glock go in the direction of the Mexican shooters.

WOP! WOP! WOP! WOP! WOP! WOP! WOP!

He saw 2 more of his brothers go down, while the rest from the dice game followed his lead and started shooting back. Luccy was sticking and moving. He was taking cover behind a broke down car when he saw one of the shooter's AKs jam. He moved from behind the car and walked him down!

WOP! WOP! WOP! WOP! WOP! WOP! WOP!

He killed him. Before he could move, another Mexican popped up a foot in front of him. Luccy moved with quickness and put the barrel of the Glock under his chin and fired. WOP! WOP! Blood from his victim's face sprayed all over him and covered his gun.

THRAAATAATATAAT!

He saw the Tamale Lady kill another of his homeboys. Seeing that he was the last person from the dice game alive, he ran behind a row of cars parked on the street, taking fire from Maria and her goons.

THRAATATAAT! THRAAATAAT! THRAAATATAAT!

He could feel the glass from the car windows breaking and hitting him. He pointed his Glock behind him and started to fire blindly to give himself cover while he ran to safety, pulling the trigger 'til it clicked empty.

Maria jumped on top of a parked car—this was what she trained for!—and aimed the green beam on her MP5 at Luccy's running body and pulled the trigger... Nothing happened. She pulled the trigger again, and when it didn't fire, she looked down and seen the bullet was sideways. She smacked the lever out of frustration.

"Ahhhh!" she screamed. She got the shell unjammed and aimed again at Luccy, but he was too far and out of the range of the subcompact machine gun when she fired.

Luccy hit the corner and took off like Usain Bolt! Getting to safety was his only concern. *Who were these muthafuckas?* he thought while running. *They hadn't beefed with Mexicans in years, so what were they tripping on? Ice cream trucks and Tamale Ladies? Who the fuck were these people?* He got a half mile away, hitting all backyards, backstreets, fences, and alleys. He hid in the backyard of a bando in the outskirts of their hood.

He was waiting on an Uber to come get him and take him from Phoenix to his uncle's house in Tucson. His uncle was his OG, and with his help, he would get to the bottom of this shit!

***

"Bahado! Turn on the Phoenix news! We took out all of Los' workers today! Well, one got away, but we still hit them hard!" Maria said to Bird while they video chatted on Telegram.

"I seen it already. I'm proud of you. How do you feel after your first mission?" he asked her.

"Oh my god! Jefito, I loved it! I'm still feeling the adrenaline rush an hour later! Juan was perfect during the getaway drive. He's like a little innocent boy. Nobody would ever pull him over."

"I'm glad to hear it. Keep the pressure on them, Mari. Don't let up. What do you have planned for tomorrow?" Bird inquired.

"Juan and a couple of the guys are painting the van black right now. It should be ready to go mañana. We're going to double back on their trap. This time late night while the crackheads are out. Really shut their shit down!" she answered.

"I love the way you think. That's smart. Hit them in their pockets. It costs money to fight wars. Oh, I forgot to tell you. The men I sent to assist you? Those are your men. Loyal to you. Treat them right. My gift to you. Your first 20 soldiers. Congratulations, Mana De Jefe." Bird told her.

Maria was overwhelmed. Her own soldiers! She loved Bird for this! "Gracias, jefe! I won't let you down out here!"

"Call me tomorrow and let me know how it goes," Bird said and hung up, feeling proud of his protegé. Even though she was a woman and the Mexican cartel business was about money and masculinity, he wasn't ashamed to make her his protegé publicly.

***

Maria pulled one of the guys to the side and told him to gather the men together in the living room. She had an announcement to make. When she saw the last of her soldiers file in, she spoke up.

"Excuse me! Can I have your attention, por favor? Gracias!" Maria said to the group of men gathered in the living room. "So, as you know, my name is Maria. I was just made Mana De Jefe of La Familia, The Cartel. You now call me Mana Negra. But more than that, I have my own branch, and all of you are now under me. That means you're loyal strictly to me. You get your orders from me. If any of you have a problem with that, speak up now." She cocked her gun while she said the last part. Nobody spoke up.

"You'll see that I'm a hands-on boss. I'll be in the field with you, getting my hands dirty tambien. We took no losses today. But understand, there's people in this room with us that won't be here in the end. So make sure you watch the next man's back while I watch over all of yours. This is my second in command." She pointed to the soldier next to her, Ghost.

"You'll also listen to my chain of command. And you'll show respect to Juan. He earned it today." She said that last part looking at Juan, giving him a proud smile.

As Maria spoke to the men, she was endearing herself to them. If it came down to it, she wanted to make sure they would die for her with no hesitation. She needed these men to be loyal only to her if she was to accomplish Los' plan and remove Bird from the top spot and place herself there.

Today they had a chance to bond through combat and would have more chances throughout the week to do the same. Nothing builds a bond faster than killing and almost dying with each other.

She finished her speech and answered a few questions. She was confident these men would do as told. She told the men it was time to start celebrating their W, and they followed her into the kitchen, where she started handing out beers and gave one of them stacks of meat to go start grilling. While they were busy drinking and cooking, she left the estate to go meet with Los.

***

She walked into the ghetto strip club on East Camelback. Los was sitting in the back with a drink in front of him and a naked bitch next to him, in her ear. He didn't see Maria walk up.

Maria walked over to the naked bitch and lifted her up by her hair. "Move, bitch. He's already spoken for," she said and removed her from the booth. She glared at Los after she sat down.

He laughed at her and knocked his shot back. "Mamacita! Nice of you to join me!" he said and kissed her on the cheek. "I seen that shit on the news. Y'all did y'all thing! Was it everything you trained for?" he asked her.

She looked at him and couldn't stay mad. "Papi, I loved it!" she said excitedly. "One shot, one kill. My aim was true every time. One of them got away. But that's fine, 'cause that's how legends are made. A story told by a survivor."

A fucking tamale stand... That's some good shit. You was finna use that on us, huh? And got yo whole team killed. My niggas don't be slipping in alleys, shooting dice while on the clock. So y'all finna double back tonight or tomorrow?

"Tomorrow. I'm letting my soldiers celebrate tonight. So the ones with me today are mine to keep. I'm pretty sure I earned their respect and loyalty today in the field. Which is important if we're really going to go after Bird. Speaking of which, do you have a plan for that yet?" she asked him, getting antsy just speaking about it.

"My guy flies in later tonight. I'm finna put it together with him when I go over there later. I'll have an answer for you tomorrow," he said, signaling the bartender for another shot.

"Great. 'Cause I wanna hear this great fucking plan you're putting together. Risking my life for you once again, Los," she said, taking the shot from the server intended for him.

"I got you. Today went good, didn't it? Trust me. You need these runs anyway to build trust with yo team. Yo wolves gotta respect you. Especially if you going after the Alpha. Wolves respect strength. So show no weakness in front of them. Don't hesitate for one second to kill anyone that violates you. Kuz that's when they gon' turn on you," Los told her, giving her some game. "You can train for 100 gunfights, but once that first shot bark, only the most disciplined stick to the plan. And anybody can die. Make sure it aint you."

"I feel you, papi," Maria said, loving him for making sure she stayed alive. "I gotta get back to the house. Find me another trap to hit after we double back on this one. Kay, papi?"

"I got you. I gotta go though. Walk with me to my car," Los said and stood up.

"Yeah, I'm positive it's him. He's the same nigga Stinky was arguing with at The Vault. He just got here. Y'all niggas better come avenge yo homeboy!" Stink Locc's sister said to the Crip she was on the phone with. "I'll let you know when he's getting up to leave. Hurry y'all asses up though!"

She put her phone back into her bag and walked over to where Los was sitting. She sat down next to him and started playing with his chain and rubbing her hands across his chest and stomach, to feel if he was strapped up or not.

"Damn, love. You getting kinda personal with them hands," he said to her and smiled.

"Just checking out the hardware. You new around here? I never seen you in the club before." she told him.

"I'm from around the way-way. What's up with you though? This club don't seem like yo style. You got a classy look to you," he said back to her.

"Oh yeah? What seem like my style? How about you give me yo number and we can talk about this when I'm off?"

"You gotta work for this number. Shoot me yours," he said.

She was about to give him her number, when Maria snatched her up. She thought about popping off on her, but she looked into Maria's eyes and a chill ran through her body. She damn near ran out the booth.

***

Los and Maria walked out of the strip club and were instantly hit by the dry heat. While walking to his car with Maria, a black newer Chevy Impala pulled into the parking lot and parked their car sideways in the entrance, blocking Los' exit.

Four men jumped out of the car and started firing in Los' direction.

Los heard the guns bark. He grabbed Maria and pulled her behind his Durango. "You strapped?" he asked her. She shook her head no.

He hit the alarm on his car and opened the doors. He stuck his hand under the back seat and pulled out a Baby AR-15 and handed it to Maria. He pulled out a full-sized AR-10 for himself. "You go around the front," he told her.

He poked his head around the corner of the car, drawing their fire.

BRAAAT! BRAAAT! WOP! WOP! WOP! BRAAAAT!

They didn't expect for Maria to come from the other side of the car, so they focused on killing Los. Two of them seen him poke his head out and decided to go in for the kill.

Maria was already between the Durango and the car next to it. She was kneeled down and fired into their bodies as they came into her view.

THRAATATAAT! THRAAATAAT! THRAAATATAAT!

Both of them fell down, bleeding from bullet holes in their upper bodies.

Los took his chance and bounced out from behind the Durango while Maria had their attention. He fired into the chest of one of the shooters, knocking him down. The remaining gunman saw he was the only one left and decided to fight another day. He hopped in the Impala and put it into drive.

Los seen him trying to get away and moved in for the kill. He ran up to the side of the Impala and fired into the window. The gunman had been expecting that, so he got a shot off at Los, hitting him before he died.

WOP!

The shot knocked Los off his feet and the gun out of his hands. Maria ran to him and helped him up. "Come on, papi, we gotta go! The police are coming!" Maria yelled, hearing the sirens in the distance.

She helped Los into the passenger seat of the Durango and jumped behind the wheel. She put the truck in gear and got out of the parking lot seconds later— a whole half minute before the police arrived.

She looked over at Los and started to panic at the sight of so much blood on his white tee. Tears streamed down her face. She just got him back in her life—she couldn't lose him now! He was in and out of consciousness. "Call Boogie." he told her.

"Just hold on, papi! I'm taking you to the hospital!" she cried out to him.

"No hospitals. Call Boogie," he whispered before falling back out.

Maria pulled up to Legacy Phoenix and told them she had a gunshot victim in the car.

Los' last thoughts before blacking out was *I can't believe that bitch ass nigga got me!* The last thing he saw was the lights on the ceiling as he was strapped down to a stretcher and looking up as they wheeled him into surgery.

Maria seen they took him to the back for surgery and left in the Durango. She didn't want to be there when the detectives arrived asking questions about a gunfight in East Phoenix.

***

"So let me get this straight. You felt a gun on his waist when you were talking to him?" the detective asked Star, inside the strip club.

"Yes, he was rude. I've seen him in clubs before always starting fights with other customers. I'm sure he started this too," she told the FBI agent, lying on Los.

The presence of machine guns had made the local Maricopa County sheriff's call in the FBI. When Los had taken the gunshot to the chest, he had dropped his AR-10. The police had it bagged up as evidence, hoping for fingerprints or DNA from the blood that was splashed on the stock of the gun.

"Tell your manager I'm not leaving 'til I got a copy of that surveillance," the FBI agent told Star.

"Sir, I just received word that a gunshot victim has been checked in at Legacy Phoenix just a few minutes ago. Apparently he's in critical condition and is being prepped for surgery right now."

Star listened to what the agent's partner told him about Los being in critical condition and almost couldn't contain her smile, hoping he died during surgery.

"Let's grab a copy of the surveillance footage and head out there," the agent told his partner, leaving Star standing there looking stupid. "Grab a copy of her ID and her number also. We'll need her to testify later."

Star wasn't concerned. She wasn't even old enough to work in this 21-and-over club, so they could look at her fake ID all they wanted.

***

Agent Morales and his partner, Agent Williams, arrived at the hospital 20 minutes later. They video recorded a copy of the surveillance from the strip club.

They watched as four men pulled into the parking lot and engaged a male and female in a gunfight. The footage was lowkey grainy, so they couldn't really see the faces of anyone involved too good. They were curious to see if the man in surgery was the same one that got shot running up on the Impala.

At this point, all they had was the grainy footage, so if he didn't confess to being at the crime scene, they would have to let him go.

***

They saw a nurse on the floor and asked about their gunshot victim. They were told he would be in surgery for at least a few more hours, getting fragments of the shell from off his lung and from by his heart.

He came in with no ID, and the woman that dropped him off had left soon after, so he was registered as a John Doe for the time being. They asked for the footage of the woman who had brought him in. They got it and told the nurse they would return in the morning to ask the patient a few questions.

***

Los came to, walking down a dark hallway. He was the only person on his side of the hallway. Across the hall, there were lights on the ceiling, with a line of people walking in the opposite direction of him, towards a more ambient light...

He tried to speak to a few of them but was ignored. He tried to cross the hallway over to the other side, but there was an unseen wall denying him access. Whenever he tried to stop and turn around, something unseen as well kept pushing him forward. *Was he on his way to hell?* The last thing he remembered was being shot in his chest and Maria helping him into the car. *Was he dead?* he wondered. He got to the end of the hall and there was a door. He tried to open it, and it was locked... denying him entry...

He woke up in the hospital, mouth dry and chest on fire. He looked at the clock on the wall—5:04 AM.

He looked at the table next to the bed and seen his phone on it. Thank God it wasn't dead. He grabbed it and called Boogie. After telling him not to panic, he told him what happened.

After he was done with the story, he dropped his pin and told Boogie to come right away. He didn't know if the club had cameras or not, but what he did know was he wasn't tryna stick around to answer any questions that a nosy ass detective had for him. He had no clue the FBI was already on the case.

"And brother. Don't tell LeeLee a thing! Just come on!" Los told him.

"Bro, you been gone all night. She's up worried about you. We all been. Sis probably pacing in her room right now. Kayla and Liv both in there with her. She goes from cussing you out to crying. Shit, the only thing that's gon' save you from her is you getting shot in the chest like you say!" Boogie joked.

"Nigga hurry the fuck up! I just GPS"d the house and you 38 minutes away. I'ma wait to sign out 'til you get here just in case they alert the boys. I don't wanna have nowhere to go if they do that. You feel me?" Los said.

"Bet. I'm sneaking out the door right now!" Boogie told him and hung up.

Los pressed the button for the nurse and told her he needed another pain pill. His chest was on fire! And it hurt to breathe.

He checked his phone and seen 25 minutes had passed since he talked to Boogie. He pressed the button again, and when the nurse came, he told her to bring the papers to sign. He was ready to leave.

"Chile, aint nothing in them streets worth your life. You understand me? Just stay a day or two and let your body heal," she pleaded with him, genuinely concerned.

"I appreciate the concern foreal. But I gotta go foreal. Just bring the papers please and thank you," he told her, trying his best to stay respectful to the older Black woman. His mother taught him to respect his elders—especially women of color.

"If you say so. I hope you got a ride home. You aint in no condition to be on that road behind no wheel," she said. "Young people these days aint got no sense," he heard her saying under her breath while she left to get his voluntary discharge paperwork. He laughed at that last part.

Chapter 32

Los sat in the passenger seat of Boogie's 550 Benz. He had his eyes closed, high off the perc he had taken when he got in the car.

"So you think maybe Maria lined you up, brother?" Boogie asked him. Los was snapped back to reality with that question.

"Nah... She has no reason to. And that bitch saved my life foreal. I actually need to call her and see where she at with my car. But nah. Maria is good. She wouldn't have slid on them Crip niggas earlier just to line me up right after. Doesn't make sense, you feel me?" Los told him.

"Yeah, I feel you. So what you finna tell Lee? Shit, she probably finna be mad at me for coming to get you with out telling her," Boogie said. They both laughed, kuz it was true.

"The truth. I was meeting with a client and some niggas thought I was slipping. It could be worse foreal. Half an inch lower and that bitch ass nigga would've shot me in the heart. She know what she signed up for fucking with me. I dropped the AR though when he popped me," he told Boogie, hoping Maria picked the gun up.

"I'ma slide by the club later today when it open and check the temp. See if the boys got a copy of the tape. And see how much he want for our copy," Boogie said.

"Hit Brazo and Lil Tony and tell them to keep their ears to the streets about 4 dead niggas and where they from. We need to find out why these niggas targeted me."

"Here we are," Boogie said, pulling up to the house. "Y'all bedroom light still on. They still up!" They both started laughing.

Before he turned the car off, Kaleah was running out of the house, cussing Los out. She got to the passenger side of the car and ripped the car door open.

"Nigga explain your fucking self!" she said, reaching in and grabbing his shoulders.

"Ahhh," Los said, wincing at the pain.

Kaleah heard this and finally looked down at him in the car and seen the bandages across his chest and the hospital tag on his wrist.

"Oh my God, babe! What the fuck happened?" she screamed at him. Los was still out of breath from her grabbing him. "Boogie, what the fuck happened to my fiancé?" she yelled over the car to him.

"Bro got shot in the chest last night. When he wasn't picking up his phone, he was at the hospital, in surgery. An inch lower and the bullet would've hit him in the heart. He called me to pick him up kuz he didn't want you to panic. Now help me get him inside," he told her.

"Oh my God, baby! I'm so sorry! Are you okay?" she said to Los, breaking down into tears.

"Yeah baby. Just help me out the car and into the house." She moved out the way so Boogie could pull him out of the car, then she helped him into the house. He had an arm around each of their shoulders as he walked from the driveway into the house.

They got inside and led him into the back living room, where the big sectional couch was, and helped him sit down. Boogie went back to the car to grab Los' medicine. Kaleah was still crying.

Liv and Kayla heard her crying and came downstairs fast, thinking that Los had broke her heart. They saw the bandages across his chest and knew something bad had happened.

"Brother, you good?" Liv asked him.

Los' chest and lungs were on fire. He couldn't speak, so he raised a hand to her, letting her know he was good.

"Sister, my nigga almost died. An inch lower and the bullet would've hit him in the heart!" Just saying those words had LeeLee crying even more.

"Who did this to you, Los?" Kayla asked him at the same time Boogie was coming back into the room. She looked at him for an answer.

"He was just in surgery a few hours ago. He should still be at the hospital, but the police was finna be back with questions, so this is the best place for him to be. Let's leave him alone with the questions and let him rest. The niggas that did this are dead. It's nothing to worry about," Boogie told the three women in the room, crowding his brother.

"How can you say there's nothing to worry about, Ace? Just look at him! He's in pain! He was shot! I know what that feels like and it doesn't feel great!" Kaleah cried out.

"I can say that kuz my brother is alive. Let's be thankful for that instead of crying about him being shot. Y'all know what comes with fucking with a street nigga. That could be me right there and Kayla in your place, Lee. Bro is alive. That's all that matters," Boogie said, grabbing Kayla's arm, pulling her towards the stairs.

"Sis, I'ma be in my room if you need me. I love you, brother. Hope you feel better," Liv said and left out the room and up the stairs.

Later that day, Boogie left the house with a few things on his to-do list. Since Los was laid up, he decided to bring Kayla with him. Los supported it, especially after hearing how she smoked her old FBI partner. She was ice cold. He fucked with it!

Their first stop was the strip club on East Camelback. They went inside and ordered drinks. The topic of conversation throughout the club was the shootout in the parking lot yesterday.

A stripper named Star seemed to know more about it than the other bitches, so Boogie put Kayla on her while he tried to finesse the bartender into letting him record the footage on his phone.

Kayla was getting a lap dance from Star when she asked, "Where you working yesterday when the shooting happened? Oh my God, I couldn't imagine being here with all that going on so close!" she said, and slipped a $20 into Star's g-string.

"Girl, was I! That was nothing! Niggas be shooting in my hood all the time. Matter fact, I know them niggas who pulled up and started shooting! That light-skin nigga that almost died killed my brother Stink Locc! Or at least that's what the streets is saying!" Star told her while grinding her body on Kayla's lap.

"Foreal? That's so crazy! So you seen him and called your brother's homeboys?" Kayla asked her.

"You asking a lot of questions! But between me and you? Let's just say I was mad when I found out he lived! I mean, they all died trying to kill this one skinny ass nigga! But his bitch helped him too! Nobody was expecting that!" Star said, shaking her head in disappointment.

"His bitch? What do you mean?" Kayla asked her, while slipping another $20 in her g-string.

"Yeah! His bitch killed everyone! It was some Mr. and Mrs. Smith shit foreal!" Star said, getting up from Kayla's lap because the song was over. "But hey, I get off at midnight tonight. Link with me later?" she told Kayla and asked for her phone so she could lock her number in.

After she had the number, Kayla went back to the bar where Boogie was and asked him if he was having any luck with the bartender and the footage.

"I gave her a blue face for it, but I got it. You ready to dip?" he asked her.

"Yeah, I got something crazy to tell you in the car anyway," she told him, then followed him outside to the Benz.

They got in, and Boogie pulled up the footage from the shooting, and they watched it together for the first time. There indeed was a woman there who saved Los' ass. Who was she?

"Who is that girl with him, Ace? And don't lie for your friend either," she told him, looking him in his eyes.

"Shit, yo guess is as good as mine," he lied to her face. "What's that something krazy you gotta tell me though?" he asked her.

"Oh shit! I almost forgot! So the girl who was giving me the lap dance? I asked her what happened yesterday and she hinted that she set the whole thing up! She said Los killed her brother Stink Locc—I assume he's a Crip? So she saw Los in the club and plotted some get back. What do you want to do? She also said his bitch killed everyone and saved him. She also gave me her number and said her shift ends at midnight. So what do you want to do?"

"It's only one thing we can do," Boogie told her. "But I'm finna call Los first and let him know this new development. This answers a few questions though about who and why."

He called Los and got him on the fifth ring. "Brother! Sorry to bother you, but I got some shit you wanna hear," Boogie told him.

"And what's that?" Los asked him.

"So I guess this lil bitch that works at the club on Camelback is saying you smoked her brother Stink Locc, and she recognized you at the club, so she called his homeboys and told them you was there. So they slid up there, and you know what happened after that."

Now this definitely was something he wanted to hear. "Is that right?" he said, slightly slurring his words kuz of the percs. "Who is this bitch? You know she can't live right, brother."

"I figured you would say that. Her name is Star. She don't get off for some hours though, but don't trip, it's gon' be taken care of. I'm finna slid by and see what Brazo talking 'bout next."

"Yup. Let me know what niggas is saying. Call Lil Tony and tell him to bring that nurse bitch he fucks with to the house. I need my bandages changed by a professional. We can pay her whatever. It's good," Los told him.

"I got you. I'm finna hit niggas right now," Boogie said and hung up.

He looked at Kayla and said, "You ready to go on a mission tonight? This shit should be easier than smoking an FBI agent." Boogie said, starting the car and pulling out of the parking lot.

"If shit gotta get handled correctly, have a woman do it. Of course I'm down, babe. Duh," she joked and reached over the center console, grabbing his hand into hers. "I wonder if the FBI was called to come and investigate since it was machine guns involved? While you go meet with Brazo, drop me off at the office so I can see what the word is," she told him.

Kayla was technically still an FBI agent. The only person who knew about her being in Arizona was Malone, and he was dead. So for the time being, she was still able to go into the office and log in and see what the word was. She could log in from her laptop, but she wouldn't be able to check the temp and see what other agents were saying. So she still preferred to go in.

"That's a good idea. I got you. Hit me when you almost done though so I can pull up when you are done. You feel me? After that shit with yo old partner, I don't want you in that building any longer than you have to be," he said and reached over and rubbed her belly. Even though she wasn't showing yet, this act brought both of them comfort.

Boogie dropped her off and made his way to the trap. He had to see what the numbers were looking like. Then he would pull up on Brazo and see what the streets were saying.

***

Boogie got off the phone with Lil Tony, giving him instructions to bring the nurse bitch to the house to help change Los' bandages. He hung up and got out of the car. He walked up to where Brazo and his 79 Swan homies were politicking.

Brazo seen him walking up and stood up to greet him. "Boogie, ma blooda. How's Brody doing?" Brazo said, checking up on Los. He had seen enough people get shot in the chest to know that the first few days were tricky.

"He good. Just resting and tryna heal up. You know how bro is, he tryna get back outside asap! Appreciate the concern though, whoop."

"No doubt. Los is a solid nigga. Y'all niggas came in to town and been showing love on the packs, I gotta reciprocate. Them dead niggas was from North Phoenix though. They hood is a branch of Charity Homes. They be on 44th in them blue joints I told y'all about awhile back," Brazo said, while lighting a Backwood. He hit it and passed it to Boogie.

Boogie hit the blunt and thought about what Brazo just told him. "So I guess this lil stripper bitch recognized bro in the club and called them niggas. You said them joints on 44th though? Good look, whoopty," he said and handed the blunt back to Brazo.

"Anytime ma nigga. Let me know if you need niggas to slide out there with y'all. I been waiting to get on them sucka niggas anyway!" Brazo told him.

"I got you, Blood. I'ma let you know what's good. I'm finna get in the wind though. Y'all niggas stay dangerous!" Boogie said and walked back to his Benz and got in. He texted Kayla he was on the way and started his car, heading back to the FBI field office.

***

Kayla was logging off the computer when an agent she didn't recognize walked in.

"I've been seeing you around the office a few times and never had the chance to introduce myself. My name is Mike Morales. Special Agent in Charge. What field office are you out of?" he asked her.

Kayla didn't panic. She knew there were no ties between her and Malone's murder, so she answered truthfully.

"I'm out of the Portland office. Been undercover awhile out here. I stop by to check in online with my chain of command and to see what the word is," she told him, sizing him up.

"I see, I see. You said Portland? Didn't one of your field operatives get murdered recently?" Agent Morales asked her.

Kayla didn't break a sweat. "Yes, unfortunately. He was my partner awhile back before I started the mission I'm on right now. How'd you guys hear about that all the way down here?"

"The FBI is a small world. I actually knew Agent Malone. Good man. I read his notes after he died, and he had taken an interest in some people that just moved out here. We actually just matched one of their DNA to a gun found at the scene of a shooting yesterday. The trail stops cold there though. He checked out of the hospital a few hours after surgery and left no forwarding address. Imagine that! A shot to the chest and he leaves the hospital. Must have something major to hide... We were going to question him today. But no worries. We'll catch up to him. We always do, you know."

"Wow, that is so crazy. The world is definitely small. Well, good luck on your case. I gotta go. When I'm gone too long my people start asking questions," Kayla said and moved to walk out the door.

Agent Morales put a hand on her shoulder, stopping her. "Here, take my card. If you ever need anything while you're out here, give me a ring," he said and handed her his card.

She took it and told him, "Will do," and walked out of the room, anxious to be out of the building. Boogie was there when she walked out of the lobby into the evening sun.

Morales watched her leave the building and get into a waiting Benz and pull off. He also seen her drop his card as soon as she got outside. Something was off about this woman and he was going to find out.

She got in and said, "We have a problem," then told him everything Agent Morales had told her, leaving out no detail.

Boogie said nothing for a few moments while he thought about what she just dropped in his lap. *Fuck! They got bro's DNA from that gun he dropped!* he thought. "Is there any way you can get that gun?" he asked her.

"Babe what! No! They'll have that gun locked away and only Morales and his partner will be able to get it released. I felt weird when he was talking to me. Like he could see through me. Especially when he brought up Malone being killed. Oooh I get the heebie jeebies just thinking about it," she said, tryna shake off the feeling that she just got thinking about the conversation she had with the other agent.

"Well we gotta let bro know what's up. He has a new set of fingerprints. The only way they could get that DNA is through his blood. He won't be happy to hear this. The one thing money couldn't replace. Fuck!" Boogie said, pounding his fist on the steering wheel.

"It's gonna be dark in a couple hours though babe. Let's get ready for the mission tonight and deal with all that later when we get home. We gotta focus. That's how we don't get caught, remember?" Kayla said, quoting Boogie with the last part.

He looked at her and smiled. "You right. Let's go smoke this bitch."

***

Kayla texted Star: *"Hey girl! Wya?"* While she waited for her to reply, she screwed the titanium suppressor onto the polymer Ghost Glock.

Boogie looked at his babymom with pride.

Star texted back: *"Just getting off. Finna go home. Come over!"*

Kayla: *"Addy?"*

Star: *"3912 N 39th Ave. Apt 202"*

Kayla: *"See you in 30!"*

Kayla gave Boogie the address and they drove there in the Benz. They were 10 minutes away when he parked the car and told her to wait for him. He got out, and after having small difficulty choosing which one, he stole a newer Kia Optima. He pulled up next to the Benz, and Kayla got out and hopped in the stoley.

They pulled up to Star's apartment complex and Kayla looked at Boogie and said, "You coming?"

"Yeah I'll rock with you. Pass me the pole." She handed him the gun and they got out and walked to apartment 202, making sure to keep their heads down in case there were cameras on the building. They reached 202 and Kayla knocked.

Boogie stood at the bottom of the stairs. The plan was for Kayla to go in and leave the door unlocked. Boogie was to go in 2 minutes after her and shoot Star.

Kayla knocked and was let in to the one-bedroom apartment. She left the door unlocked for Boogie.

Star was slow dancing in the kitchen, drinking from a bottle of Casa Migos while *"Jodeci"* was playing on the Bluetooth speaker. There were candles burning and the lights were dim. If Kayla hadn't been there to kill the girl, she would definitely be feeling the vibe.

Star slow danced her way over to Kayla and offered her the bottle after taking one last sip.

Kayla set it on the counter while Star turned around and started looking through the cupboards for shot glasses.

Kayla picked the bottle back up and put the lid on it. She saw Star was turned around rummaging through the cupboards still. She turned the bottle upside down and cracked Star over the head with it. *HARD!*

The bottle didn't break, so Kayla kept hitting her with it 'til it did, drenching Star's face and Kayla's hands with tequila.

Boogie walked in and seen Kayla squatting over a laid-out Star, stabbing her in the face and throat with the broken bottle. "Bitch you gonna set up my family! Bitch!" Kayla was screaming while Star's blood was spraying all over the front of her. Kayla didn't care though, she was in a place only killing brought her.

After watching this for 30 seconds and seeing that Star was obviously dead, he calmly said, "Babe. Come on, we gotta go," not wanting to touch her while she was in the zone and have her accidentally stab him.

Kayla shook out of it when she heard his voice and looked down at her hands and the front of her body—covered in blood.

Boogie opened the cabinet under the sink and pulled out a black Glad bag. He grabbed the broken bottle shards from the floor and Kayla's hands, putting them in the trash bag. He grabbed a long piece of glass sticking out of Star's neck and put that in the bag also. "Come on baby, let's dip," he said to her and grabbed Star's phone. It was an Android, so he took the SIM card out and stomped on the phone, breaking it before they left just as silently as they came in. He locked the bottom lock on the way out.

He gave Kayla his hoodie to wear and put her blood-soaked hoodie in the bag with the glass shards. They got back to the stolen Kia and drove the 10 minutes back to Boogie's Benz. He kept a gallon of gas in the trunk for shit just like this.

He soaked her hoodie and the Glad bag in gas and lit it on fire. Kayla sat in the car while Boogie watched 'til the contents of the bag were engulfed in flames. When he was sure they were destroyed, he started the car and left. He wasn't worried about anyone calling the police about arson. This was an alley in North Phoenix. Shit was on fire all the time!

Chapter 33

Boogie checked in with Los when he got home, telling him about what happened at Star's apartment and about the conversation Kayla had with the other FBI agent. Los was coherent, barely. This conversation would have to happen in the morning.

Lil Tony had brought his nurse bitch over to change his bandages. While she was there she taught Kaleah and Liv the basics so they could do it the next time he needed them changed.

The biggest part right now was avoiding infection. If a wound that close to his heart got infected, it was almost fatal every time.

Caesar had checked in when his plane landed, expecting Los to come over to the Villa. When he found out Los was shot he insisted that he come over there. They were expecting him any minute. Los had Boogie help him go down the stairs to the basement.

10 minutes later Caesar showed up with Dolce. They were shocked at Los' condition. They wondered why he wasn't at a hospital but respected his decision after learning why he left.

Regardless of being shot or not, after a few minutes of them being overly concerned about his condition, Los got straight to business: putting Maria in Bird's spot.

"So tell me about this Maria," Caesar said.

"She's capable. She's highly trained for the top spot and she saved my life yesterday. She has her own men, loyal only to her. From what I've seen of her in action; with our help it shouldn't be too hard knocking Bird off the chess board. With her in his spot that puts her in our pocket. With her support we could make our Organization one of the top 4 families," Los told him.

"Hmmm. I definitely like the sound of that. You're certain she's capable of biting the hand that's feeding her? Don't you worry about her turning on you if she's so quick to kill Bird?" Caesar asked.

"Nah. I was the hand that fed her first. This is my day one. I wouldn't be vouching for no silly bitch. Trust me. This is a power move foreal. Just think about the power you'd have with a whole nother Cartel in your pocket? The new smuggling routes you'd have access to. The extra network is worth working with her alone! An ally that would never forget you placed her in power," Los spoke with energy in his voice, he was convinced this was the right move and would put his all behind it.

Dolce had sat back this whole time and said nothing. As her man's advisor it wasn't her place to speak but to listen. And what she just listened to made her speak up.

"Jefe," she said to Caesar. "I think this is a power move *tambien*. Los is right."

Caesar looked at her while she said this and knew Dolce would never lead him astray. If her analytical mind thought this was the right move, he believed it.

"So how do we make this happen? I assume you got a strategy ready for me to hear?" Caesar asked Los.

"I thought you'd never ask," Los said and smiled. "We use her relationship with Bird to infiltrate his compound. With 20 men loyal to her and us backing her, we should be able to overpower whatever resistance his men will put up. We find out how many men he has working the compound. We hit it early in the morning. We have Maria in place inside the night before. When she lets us know he's sleeping, we have her open the gate for us. Her men will already have taken out his men by this time, so we show up for the kill shot. I already told her whatever family he has with him will have to die also. Hopefully his mother is there. Her voice has power in their organization for sure," Los finished saying, proud of his problem solving.

"I love it. I'm proud of you, Los. Even with a gunshot wound to the chest you don't fail to amaze me with your thoroughness. I'll want to meet her before we do this. Can we all meet here?" Caesar asked him.

"Uhhhh..." Boogie said, unable to form a sentence, thinking about Maria in Kaleah's home.

"Noooo..." Los answered, dragging out the word. "This spot aint for her. I gotta keep my family separate from all this. I hope you understand. But we'll have to meet at a neutral spot. I'll rent a suite at the Hyatt in downtown Scottsdale. Have her meet us there. Give me a few days and we'll do it."

"Then we're all set," Caesar said, standing up. "I'll call you tomorrow and check on you. Gotta keep the Alpha of my Wolf Pack alive." After he said this, he embraced Los and Boogie showed them the way out.

Dolce peeked her head back around the staircase and told him to stay alive. *The Game needs you.* Then she followed behind Caesar and Boogie up the stairs.

Boogie came back down to the basement after they left and sat down on the couch across from him. "Yo plan is thorough whoopty. Can't deny that. If we do this though and place yo old bitch at the head of the Sinaloa Cartel then we're setting ourselves up for a major come up. Maria gon' be in yo pocket for life... Shiiit, she'll owe you her whole life. If she reciprocates like we think she will then we're set. But what if that bitch is ungrateful? Then what? We kill her and replace her with who? You?" Boogie asked, picking his brother's brain.

"See brother... Y'all don't know her like I do. Our history finna guarantee that she show love back to us. With her at the top spot, as long as I give her some dick every now and then we'll be good. It's when she not getting fucked that she trips out on me," Los told him.

"Well make sure you dicking that Krazy bitch down, brother!" Boogie joked, causing Los to hurt his lung laughing so hard.

"On me! That bitch will get to tweaking foreal!" Los said.

"You finna stay down here, brother? I'm finna head up to the room with Kay," Boogie told him.

"Yeah, I'm good, bro. Go do yo thang," Los told him, twisting up a backwood. Kapone had just come back from the town Portland with a pound of Gelato for him. Tree in Arizona was sticks and stems! Trash!

Since being shot, everybody in his presence was hovering all over him. He appreciated the concern but definitely appreciated the solitude the basement and this blunt was about to offer him.

He sparked up and blew out a cloud of smoke. The blunt mixed with the perc had him on cloud 9. Besides being shot in the chest, everything else in his life was progressing forward just like he had planned it.

By the time the backwood was a roach, Los' eyes were so heavy he could barely keep them open. He set the roach in the ashtray and kicked his feet up. He closed his eyes and was asleep instantly, at peace with everything going on.

Little did he know his immediate future was going to be filled with life or death moments for everybody around him.

TO BE CONTINUED

Lock Down Publications and Ca$h Presents Assisted Publishing Packages

Due to an increase in the price of services we have increased our prices. The prices below reflect the price increase as of 11/1/24.

BASIC PACKAGE **$699** Editing Cover Design Formatting	**UPGRADED PACKAGE** **$1000** Typing Editing Cover Design Formatting Upload eBooks to Amazon Upload Paperback to Amazon
ADVANCE PACKAGE **$1,400** Typing Editing (line editing/content) Cover Design Formatting Copyright Registration Proofreading Upload eBooks to Amazon Upload Paperback to Amazon	**LDP SUPREME PACKAGE** **$1,700** Typing Editing (line editing/content) Cover Design Formatting Copyright Registration Proofreading Set up Amazon Account Upload eBooks to Amazon Upload Paperback to Amazon Advertise on LDP's Amazon and Facebook Page

***

Other services available upon request.
Additional charges may apply

Lock Down Publications
P.O. Box 944
Stockbridge, GA 30281-9998
Phone: 470 303-9761
Email: lockdownpublications@gmail.com

Submission Guideline

Submit the first three chapters of your completed manuscript to ldpsubmissions@gmail.com. In the subject line add **Your Book's Title**. The manuscript must be in a Word Doc file and sent as an attachment. Document should be in Times New Roman, double spaced, and in size 12 font. Also, provide your synopsis and full contact information. If sending multiple submissions, they must each be in a separate email.

Have a story but no way to send it electronically? You can still submit to LDP/Ca$h Presents. Send in the first three chapters, written or typed, of your completed manuscript to:

LDP: Submissions Dept
P.O. Box 944
Stockbridge, GA 30281-9998

DO NOT send original manuscript. Must be a duplicate.
Provide your synopsis and a cover letter containing your full contact information.

Thanks for considering LDP and Ca$h Presents.

NEW RELEASES

BLOODLINE OF A SAVAGE 1-3
THESE VICIOUS STREETS 1-3
RELENTLESS GOON 1-3
BY PRINCE A. TAUHID

THE BUTTERFLY MAFIA 1-3
BY FUMIYA PAYNE

A THUG'S STREET PRINCESS 1&2
BY MEESHA

CITY OF SMOKE 3
BY MOLOTTI

GET IT IN SLUGS 1 &2
BY B. STALL

STANDING ON HER BUSINESS 1&2
BY DG SANTANA

STEPPERS 1,2&3
THE REAL BADDIES OF CHI-RAQ
BY KING RIO

THE LANE 1&2
BY KEN-KEN SPENCE

THUG OF SPADES 1&2
LOVE IN THE TRENCHES 2
CORNER BOYS
BY COREY ROBINSON

TIL DEATH 3
BY ARYANNA

THE BIRTH OF A GANGSTER 4
BY DELMONT PLAYER

PRODUCT OF THE STREETS 1-3
BY DEMOND "MONEY" ANDERSON

NO TIME FOR ERROR
BY KEESE

MONEY HUNGRY DEMONS 1-2
BY TRANAY ADAMS

HUB CITY MENACE 1-3
BY J. WHITE

A THUGGISH PASSION 1&2
LAND OF DA HOOLIGANZ 1-4
KILLAZ ON STANDBY 1&2
BY IRA B.

FO'EVA ROLLIN 1&2
BY ASSA RAYMOND BAKER

THE LEVEL UP 1&3
BY LUXURY KING

Coming Soon from Lock Down Publications/Ca$h Presents

IF YOU CROSS ME ONCE 6
ANGEL V
By Anthony Fields

A THUGS STREET PRINCESS 3
By Meesha

CORNER BOYS 2
By Corey Robinson

THA TAKEOVER
By Keith Chandler

BETRAYAL OF A G 2
By Ray Vinci

SAVAGE FAMILY EMPIRE 1&2
SOULLESS GOON 1,2&3
THE DIRTY SIDE OF MONEY 1,2&3
By Prince

FOR MY ENEMY'S SAKE
AMBITIONS OF A SLIDER
FRESH OFF DA PORCH
By IRA B.

THE TRUCKLOAD 1-4
TIPPIN' THE SCALES 1-3
BAD BITCHES WIT GUNZ 3
PROBLEM SOLVED 2
By Christopher "Diesel" Hornezes

Available Now

RESTRAINING ORDER 1 & 2
By **CA$H & Coffee**

LOVE KNOWS NO BOUNDARIES 1-3
By **Coffee**

RAISED AS A GOON I, II, III & IV
BRED BY THE SLUMS I, II, III
BLAST FOR ME I & II
ROTTEN TO THE CORE I II III
A BRONX TALE I, II, III
DUFFLE BAG CARTEL I II III IV V VI
HEARTLESS GOON I II III IV V
A SAVAGE DOPEBOY I II
DRUG LORDS I II III
CUTTHROAT MAFIA I II
KING OF THE TRENCHES
By **Ghost**

LAY IT DOWN I & II
LAST OF A DYING BREED I II
BLOOD STAINS OF A SHOTTA I & II III
By **Jamaica**

LOYAL TO THE GAME I II III
LIFE OF SIN I, II III
By **TJ & Jelissa**

IF LOVING HIM IS WRONG…I & II
LOVE ME EVEN WHEN IT HURTS I II III
By **Jelissa**

PUSH IT TO THE LIMIT
By **Bre' Hayes**

STAY DANGEROUS | FOREIGN BOOMIN

BLOODY COMMAS I & II
SKI MASK CARTEL I, II & III
KING OF NEW YORK I II, III IV V
RISE TO POWER I II III
COKE KINGS I II III IV V
BORN HEARTLESS I II III IV
KING OF THE TRAP I II
By **T.J. Edwards**

WHEN THE STREETS CLAP BACK I & II III
THE HEART OF A SAVAGE I II III IV
MONEY MAFIA I II
LOYAL TO THE SOIL I II III
By **Jibril Williams**

A DISTINGUISHED THUG STOLE MY HEART I II & III
LOVE SHOULDN'T HURT I II III IV
RENEGADE BOYS 1-4
PAID IN KARMA 1-3
SAVAGE STORMS 1-3
AN UNFORESEEN LOVE 1-3
BABY, I'M WINTERTIME COLD 1-3
A THUG'S STREET PRINCESS 1&2
By **Meesha**

A GANGSTER'S CODE 1-3
A GANGSTER'S SYN 1-3
THE SAVAGE LIFE 1-3
CHAINED TO THE STREETS 1-3
BLOOD ON THE MONEY 1-3
A GANGSTA'S PAIN 1-3
BEAUTIFUL LIES AND UGLY TRUTHS
CHURCH IN THESE STREETS
By **J-Blunt**

CUM FOR ME 1-8
An LDP Erotica Collaboration

BLOOD OF A BOSS 1-5
SHADOWS OF THE GAME
TRAP BASTARD
By **Askari**

THE STREETS BLEED MURDER 1-3
THE HEART OF A GANGSTA 1-3
By **Jerry Jackson**

WHEN A GOOD GIRL GOES BAD
By **Adrienne**

THE COST OF LOYALTY 1-3
By **Kweli**

BRIDE OF A HUSTLA 1-3
THE FETTI GIRLS 1-3
CORRUPTED BY A GANGSTA 1-4
BLINDED BY HIS LOVE
THE PRICE YOU PAY FOR LOVE 1-3
DOPE GIRL MAGIC 1-3
By **Destiny Skai**

A KINGPIN'S AMBITION
A KINGPIN'S AMBITION II
I MURDER FOR THE DOUGH
By **Ambitious**

TRUE SAVAGE 1-7
DOPE BOY MAGIC 1-3
MIDNIGHT CARTEL 1-3
CITY OF KINGZ 1&2
NIGHTMARE ON SILENT AVE
THE PLUG OF LIL MEXICO 1&2
CLASSIC CITY
By **Chris Green**

A GANGSTER'S REVENGE 1-4
THE BOSS MAN'S DAUGHTERS 1-5
A SAVAGE LOVE 1&2
BAE BELONGS TO ME 1&2
A HUSTLER'S DECEIT 1-3
WHAT BAD BITCHES DO 1-3
SOUL OF A MONSTER 1-3
KILL ZONE
A DOPE BOY'S QUEEN 1-3
TIL DEATH 1-3
IMMA DIE BOUT MINE 1-6
DYING FOR LIKES
By **Aryanna**

A DOPEBOY'S PRAYER
By **Eddie "Wolf" Lee**

THE KING CARTEL 1-3
By **Frank Gresham**

THESE NIGGAS AIN'T LOYAL 1-3
By **Nikki Tee**

GANGSTA SHYT 1-3
By **CATO**

THE ULTIMATE BETRAYAL
By **Phoenix**

BOSS'N UP 1-3
By **Royal Nicole**

I LOVE YOU TO DEATH
By **Destiny J**

I RIDE FOR MY HITTA
I STILL RIDE FOR MY HITTA
By **Misty Holt**

LOVE & CHASIN' PAPER
By **Qay Crockett**

TO DIE IN VAIN
SINS OF A HUSTLA
By **ASAD**

BROOKLYN HUSTLAZ
By **Boogsy Morina**

BROOKLYN ON LOCK 1 & 2
By **Sonovia**

GANGSTA CITY
By **Teddy Duke**

A DRUG KING AND HIS DIAMOND 1-3
A DOPEMAN'S RICHES
HER MAN, MINE'S TOO 1&2
CASH MONEY HO'S
THE WIFEY I USED TO BE 1&2
PRETTY GIRLS DO NASTY THINGS
By **Nicole Goosby**

LIPSTICK KILLAH 1-3
CRIME OF PASSION 1-3
FRIEND OR FOE 1-3
By **Mimi**

TRAPHOUSE KING 1-3
KINGPIN KILLAZ 1-3
STREET KINGS 1&2
PAID IN BLOOD 1&2
CARTEL KILLAZ 1-3
DOPE GODS 1&2
By **Hood Rich**

THE STREETS ARE CALLING
By **Duquie Wilson**

STEADY MOBBN' 1-3
THE STREETS STAINED MY SOUL 1-3
By **Marcellus Allen**

WHO SHOT YA 1-3
SON OF A DOPE FIEND 1-4
HEAVEN GOT A GHETTO 1&2
SKI MASK MONEY 1&2
By **Renta**

GORILLAZ IN THE BAY 1-4
TEARS OF A GANGSTA 1/&2
3X KRAZY 1&2
STRAIGHT BEAST MODE 1&2
By **DE'KARI**

TRIGGADALE 1-3
MURDA WAS THE CASE 1-3
By **Elijah R. Freeman**

SLAUGHTER GANG 1-3
RUTHLESS HEART 1-3
By **Willie Slaughter**

GOD BLESS THE TRAPPERS 1-3
THESE SCANDALOUS STREETS 1-3
FEAR MY GANGSTA 1-5
THESE STREETS DON'T LOVE NOBODY 1-2
BURY ME A G 1-5
A GANGSTA'S EMPIRE 1-4
THE DOPEMAN'S BODYGAURD 1&2
THE REALEST KILLAZ 1-3
THE LAST OF THE OGS 1-3
By **Tranay Adams**

MARRIED TO A BOSS 1-3
By **Destiny Skai & Chris Green**

KINGZ OF THE GAME 1-7
CRIME BOSS 1-4
By **Playa Ray**

FUK SHYT
By **Blakk Diamond**

DON'T F#CK WITH MY HEART 1&2
By **Linnea**

ADDICTED TO THE DRAMA 1-3
IN THE ARM OF HIS BOSS
By **Jamila**

LOYALTY AIN'T PROMISED 1&2
By **Keith Williams**

YAYO 1-4
A SHOOTER'S AMBITION 1&2
BRED IN THE GAME
By **S. Allen**

TRAP GOD 1-3
RICH $AVAGE 1-3
MONEY IN THE GRAVE 1-3
CARTEL MONEY 1&2
By **Martell Troublesome Bolden**

FOREVER GANGSTA 1&2
GLOCKS ON SATIN SHEETS 1&2
By **Adrian Dulan**

TOE TAGZ 1-4
LEVELS TO THIS SHYT 1&2
IT'S JUST ME AND YOU
By **Ah'Million**

STAY DANGEROUS | FOREIGN BOOMIN

KINGPIN DREAMS 1-3
RAN OFF ON DA PLUG
By **Paper Boi Rari**

THE STREETS MADE ME 1-3
By **Larry D. Wright**

CONFESSIONS OF A GANGSTA 1-4
CONFESSIONS OF A JACKBOY 1-3
CONFESSIONS OF A HITMAN
CONFESSIONS OF A DOPE BOY
By **Nicholas Lock**

I'M NOTHING WITHOUT HIS LOVE
SINS OF A THUG
TO THE THUG I LOVED BEFORE
A GANGSTA SAVED XMAS
IN A HUSTLER I TRUST
By **Monet Dragun**

QUIET MONEY 1-3
THUG LIFE 1-3
EXTENDED CLIP 1&2
A GANGSTA'S PARADISE
By **Trai'Quan**

CAUGHT UP IN THE LIFE 1-3
THE STREETS NEVER LET GO 1-3
By **Robert Baptiste**

NEW TO THE GAME 1-3
MONEY, MURDER & MEMORIES 1-3
By **Malik D. Rice**

CREAM 2-3
THE STREETS WILL TALK
By **Yolanda Moore**

THE STREETS WILL NEVER CLOSE 1-3
By **K'ajji**

LIFE OF A SAVAGE 1-4
A GANGSTA'S QUR'AN 1-4
MURDA SEASON 1-3
GANGLAND CARTEL 1-3
CHI'RAQ GANGSTAS 1-4
KILLERS ON ELM STREET 1-3
JACK BOYZ N DA BRONX 1-3
A DOPEBOY'S DREAM 1-3
JACK BOYS VS DOPE BOYS 1-3
COKE GIRLZ
COKE BOYS
SOSA GANG 1&2
BRONX SAVAGES
BODYMORE KINGPINS
BLOOD OF A GOON
By **Romell Tukes**

CONCRETE KILLA 1-3
VICIOUS LOYALTY 1-3
BLOODY MONEY BAGS
By **Kingpen**

THE ULTIMATE SACRIFICE 1-6
KHADIFI
IF YOU CROSS ME ONCE 1-3
ANGEL 1-4
IN THE BLINK OF AN EYE
By **Anthony Fields**

THE LIFE OF A HOOD STAR
By **Ca$h & Rashia Wilson**

NIGHTMARES OF A HUSTLA 1-3
BLOOD AND GAMES 1&2
By **King Dream**

GHOST MOB
By **Stilloan Robinson**

HARD AND RUTHLESS 1&2
MOB TOWN 251
THE BILLIONAIRE BENTLEYS 1-3
REAL G'S MOVE IN SILENCE
By **Von Diesel**

MOB TIES 1-7
SOUL OF A HUSTLER, HEART OF A KILLER 1-3
GORILLAZ IN THE TRENCHES
OOPS CRY TOO 1&2
THE DAUGHTER OF A CARTEL BOSS
By **SayNoMore**

BODYMORE MURDERLAND 1-3
THE BIRTH OF A GANGSTER 1-4
By **Delmont Player**

FOR THE LOVE OF A BOSS 1&2
By **C. D. Blue**

KILLA KOUNTY 1-5
TENDER
By **Khufu**

MOBBED UP 1-4
THE BRICK MAN 1-5
THE COCAINE PRINCESS 1-10
STEPPERS 1-3
SUPER GREMLIN 1-4
A GANGSTA'S SON
By **King Rio**

MONEY GAME 1&2
By **Smoove Dolla**

A GANGSTA'S KARMA 1-5
By **FLAME**

KING OF THE TRENCHES 1-3
By **GHOST & TRANAY ADAMS**

BAD BITCHES WIT GUNZ 1&2
PROBLEM SOLVED
By "Christopher Diesel" Hornezes

QUEEN OF THE ZOO 1&2
By **Black Migo**

GRIMEY WAYS 1-3
BETRAYAL OF A G
By **Ray Vinci**

XMAS WITH AN ATL SHOOTER
By **Ca$h & Destiny Skai**

KING KILLA 1&2
By **Vincent "Vitto" Holloway**

BETRAYAL OF A THUG 1&2
By **Fre$h**

COUNTDOWN OF A KILLA 1&2
SEX, MURDER AND GOD 1&2
GUNS DOWN, BOTTOMS UP 1&2
By Lo-Life

THE MURDER QUEENS 1-7
By **Michael Gallon**

FOR THE LOVE OF BLOOD 1-4
By **Jamel Mitchell**

HOOD CONSIGLIERE 1&2
NO TIME FOR ERROR
By **Keese**

PROTÉGÉ OF A LEGEND 1,2&3
LOVE IN THE TRENCHES 1&2
By **Corey Robinson**

THE PLUG'S RUTHLESS DAUGHTER 1&2
By **Tony Daniels**

BORN IN THE GRAVE 1-3
CRIME PAYS
By **Self Made Tay**

MOAN IN MY MOUTH
By **XTASY**

TORN BETWEEN A GANGSTER AND A GENTLEMAN
By **J-BLUNT & Miss Kim**

LOYALTY IS EVERYTHING 1-3
CITY OF SMOKE 1-3
By **Molotti**

HERE TODAY GONE TOMORROW 1&2
By **Fly Rock**

WOMEN LIE MEN LIE 1-4
FIFTY SHADES OF SNOW 1-3
STACK BEFORE YOU SPLURGE
GIRLS FALL LIKE DOMINOES
NAÏVE TO THE STREETS
By **ROY MILLIGAN**

PILLOW PRINCESS
By **S. Hawkins**

THE BUTTERFLY MAFIA 1-3
SALUTE MY SAVAGERY 1&2
By **Fumiya Payne**

THE LANE 1&2
By Ken-Ken Spence

THE PUSSY TRAP 1-5
By **Nene Capri**

DIRTY DNA
By **Blaque**

SANCTIFIED AND HORNY
by **XTASY**

BOOKS BY LDP'S CEO, CA$H

TRUST IN NO MAN
TRUST IN NO MAN 2
TRUST IN NO MAN 3
BONDED BY BLOOD
SHORTY GOT A THUG
THUGS CRY
THUGS CRY 2
THUGS CRY 3
TRUST NO BITCH
TRUST NO BITCH 2
TRUST NO BITCH 3
TIL MY CASKET DROPS
RESTRAINING ORDER
RESTRAINING ORDER 2
IN LOVE WITH A CONVICT
LIFE OF A HOOD STAR
XMAS WITH AN ATL SHOOTER

www.ingramcontent.com/pod-product-compliance
Lightning Source LLC
LaVergne TN
LVHW020711110826
845149LV00012B/2215